Murder
at Indian
Harbour

Murder
at Indian
Harbour

Janet A Couper

iUniverse, Inc.
Bloomington

Murder at Indian Harbour

iUniverse books may be ordered through booksellers or by contacting:

iUniverse
1663 Liberty Drive
Bloomington, IN 47403
www.iuniverse.com
1-800-Authors (1-800-288-4677)

Cover image by Janet A Couper, Schooner Cove Studio www.scgallery.ca
Author image by Miriam Beach Photography www.miriambeach.com

ISBN: 978-1-4759-2321-6 (sc)
ISBN: 978-1-4759-2322-3 (ebk)

Printed in the United States of America

iUniverse rev. date: 05/29/2012

"For Pat Murphy—my inspiration, editor and friend."

CONTENTS

PROLOGUE

Beth was satisfied with her life—for the most part.

Over the two decades since her parents died, she had worked long hours maintaining her father's legacy. *Pat Murphy's Pub* had survived as a mainstay of life in the small fishing village of Indian Harbour.

Thoughts of 'what her life might have been' faded with each passing year. Now at forty-two, her only wish was for the recurrent nightmares to end.

MURDER

March 16, 2011

"Last call folks!" the bartender yelled.

The crowd began to trickle out. But Leland Boutilier stood at the bar ordering another jug of Keiths draft. Obviously he and his boys would be the last to leave the pub. The stranger slumped over and sleeping on the bar, would be a challenge. Getting him on his feet and out the door would not be pleasant.

Wednesday nights were notoriously the slowest of the week. But earlier this night, the fierce north wind swept in a flurry of activity. In lobster season when a winter storm blew, the boats stayed in the cove. After supper the crews checked their moorings. Dropping by Pat Murphy's Pub to debate the weather was a ritual for the men of Indian Harbour when a Nor'easter blew in. By eight o'clock the place was full with thirty or so thirsty patrons. Beth, the bartender and owner of the Pub, was exhausted and relieved to see this night end.

In the winter months she tended bar and waited the tables. She owned the large dockside building, a small part of which housed Pat Murphy's. Directly above, on the second floor was the Grille Café operated year round by Beth's long time neighbor. Marg Snair, the chef chatted with customers while taking and delivering their orders. The menu of home cooked meals and Marg's jovial personality contributed to the popularity of the pub.

The Harbor Inn, a refurbished century house located across the highway from Pat Murphy's, was a popular retreat throughout all seasons. Despite the emotional connection to her former childhood home, Beth did not regret selling the place. The new owners brought the property to life and soon became active members of the community.

With Peggy's Cove within walking distance, the village of Indian Harbour swelled with tourists from June to early September. Seasonal sailors seeking sheltered waters dropped anchor in calm water or tied up alongside the wharf. Beth's pub became known as the spot to have a meal, a beer or two and friendly conversation. To meet the sailors' needs she had installed shower and laundry facilities. Beth opened the remainder of the building as a weekend market for local artisans.

St Margaret's Bay, from Peggy's Cove to Bayswater, held a unique charm throughout the year. Life was simple. Traditions were understood, and respected. Regardless of the notoriously unpredictable weather, the local people loved the beauty of the Bay.

"Good Night Beth! Jimmy is here to get us. Messy guy you got left there! Let me know if you need help." Leland grinned, herding his crew out the Pub's heavy wooden door. For effect he rang the large brass bell mounted on the entryway.

"Later guys." From behind the bar, Beth waved. Under her breath she added, "You assholes."

"Buddy, get up." She leaned over and shook the man's shoulder. "Where are you staying?"

No response.

"Damn you!"

She had work to do, cash out, check stock and wash up. The thought of shouldering the weight of this man out the door was irritating. She turned up the lights and flashed them.

"Hey! Wake up!"

Outside the boys were clambering into Jimmy Moore's small bus. Jimmy was sliding the back door shut when Beth rang the bell.

Leaning out the door Beth yelled, "Jimmy, I need help."

"Hang on fellas! Back in a bit." Jimmy wasted his time telling the boys; the copious draft beer had dulled their senses.

Leland laughed as he fumbled to open his door. "Yeah Jimmy, I told her buddy at the bar was looking nasty. I'll come too." He yelled to the backseat. "You guys stay put!" His boys quieted.

Before Jimmy could object Leland jumped out of the front seat.

Approaching the motionless figure at the bar Beth understood the comment Leland made before leaving. 'Messy' was the equivalent of 'pissed himself.'

The unforgettable face on the bar was not one of an unconscious drunk. The gray waxen face, unseeing open eyes and the dark stain on the man's left side confirmed the fact that something was very wrong. Seeing dark droplets on the toes of his boots, the sticky crimson pool on the floor beneath the stool—the horror of the scene became real to Beth. She began to gag.

3

"Oh God, no!" She screamed. "Jimmy, call the cops. Leland, don't touch anything!"

She insisted that Jimmy take Leland and his crew home to Dover. She needed time to think.

By the time the RCMP arrived Beth sat alone in the Pub—with a corpse. Agreeing to be interviewed by detectives later that night, she managed to answer the officer's initial questions.

*   *   *

Into the wee hours of Thursday morning Beth was uncomfortable in the metal chairs of the RCMP detachment's interrogation room. The interviews with two detectives were video recorded. Detective Rutherford, in his sixties made no eye contact with her beyond a cursory nod when he introduced himself. Not raising his eyes from the papers before him on the desk, his questioning was rote, almost robotic. But Detective Connors, a man of about her own age presented himself more cordially an hour later.

Regardless of his more congenial demeanor, Beth recognized his first question to be the same as Rutherford's.

"Was the pub full tonight?"

"The place got real busy around eight. Locals mostly."

Pausing to take a deep breath, Beth was exhausted and needed to cut the interview short.

"Detective Connors, if your questions are to be the same as the last detective's, let me make this easy for you."

"Pardon me?"

Beth looked directly into the camera lens and said,

"No, I don't know the victim. I assumed he was staying at the Inn. Yes, some other strangers came in. I didn't take much notice. I was run off my feet. No, I can't describe them, exactly; a couple, a pretty girl vaguely familiar, and a guy that looked like a professor, who by the way bought a round for the house. Needless to say, I got busy. Furthermore, I didn't have anyone working with me. The place is small. I tend the bar and wait tables. And yes it is unusual for someone to pass out on the bar. But when that happens I leave them alone until closing. Someone usually comes to get them before then. And finally, when I saw the blood on him and figured the puddle on the floor was blood and not piss, I got Jimmy to call the cops. And no, I didn't touch a thing; I didn't move him and I didn't check for a pulse. He was dead! Any idiot could see that." Beth's voice got louder. "Can I go home now?" In truth, she was about to vomit.

"Good memory. That's all for now." The detective mistook her pallor for fatigue. "I appreciate that you're overwhelmed and that you must be tired." His demeanor softened somewhat. "Do you need a ride home?"

"I got myself here. I'm fine on my own," Beth whispered as she hurried out the door.

Indian Harbour's past did not include murder. In the winter of 2011 Pat Murphy's Pub made history, in the tiny community on the shores of St Margaret's Bay, Nova Scotia.

INTRODUCTIONS

B eth Johnston fell into bed as the sun was rising.
Even then the phone beside her bed was ringing. Reaching over she pulled the cord. She fell into a place just past consciousness. *Wind battered windows. Children, faces distorted with fear. Shrill female screams as the glass shattered.* The familiar dream jolted Beth awake, a cold sweat soaking her pillow. She got up, dressed and walked to the pub.

Yellow strips of Crime Scene tape surrounded Beth's building. A uniformed officer was posted at the door. She introduced herself. He told her the Pub would have to be closed until the investigators finished their work. She was not permitted to enter.

"And just how long will this take Officer?" Beth was both furious and relieved.

"You met Detective Connors. He's in charge. I'm sure he will call you ma'am."

"I see. Thank you." Beth turned on her heel and walked quickly home. More than the morning's freezing temperature chilled her to the bone.

Local media photographers and interviewers filled every nook and cranny of the village. Hoping to get the public reaction or the opportunity to get a story, they were disappointed. The people of Indian Harbour had lots to talk about, amongst themselves and not to nosy reporters.

*   *   *

The weather cleared and the boats went out. Life approached normal. But Beth was in a state of limbo, still in shock seeing that face. Her friends called and came by to see if she needed anything. Unable to muster the energy to be the least hospitable, those same friends became concerned for her. This was simply not Beth.

Marg Snair visited Beth on Sunday afternoon, as she faithfully did after church.

"Worried about you girl. Known you a long time."

"Really Marg, I'm OK. This mess is not good for business. Damn coroner hasn't finished and God knows when they will get that nasty tape off the place. My home phone rings off the hook with reporters wanting an interview. It will calm down. I know that."

"You call me! Don't you hide away."

Monday morning Beth's cell phone rang. Seeing the number displayed she answered, "Hello, this is Beth Johnston."

"Detective Connors here. I interviewed you last week about the murder in your establishment."

"Oh, you mean the business that I own which is losing money by the minute?"

"Ah, yes ma'am. I have an update for you. Can you come into the office?"

"Fine. As long as I can sit in a comfortable chair this time. I'll be there in an hour."

The sun was shining and the road to Tantallon was clear. Beth went through the Tim Horton's drive through and got a large double double. Parking her car in the RCMP lot she took a deep breath. More curious than confident she entered the building.

"I'm here to see Detective Connors."

"Beth, I am so sorry about what happened." Cpl Sal Walters was at the front desk. Beth recognized her from the pub.

"Thanks Sal."

"I'll get him for you."

The detective presented himself, extended his hand, "Thanks for coming in."

He led Beth to his office. Seated in a comfortable chair she sipped her coffee.

"We have identified the victim, Ms Johnston."

"Call me Beth." Setting her cup on his desk, she sat back giving him her full attention.

"Okay, Beth. I have notified his next of kin and therefore able to tell you that the victim's name was Leon Mason. We identified his fingerprints from the glass we took from the bar. He had a criminal record and was released from Dorchester Penitentiary just days before he was murdered."

"So he was a criminal. Why was he in prison?"

"Assault and rape. He served ten years."

Beth sat forward in the chair. "Does this mean I can open the pub now?"

"Yes, the tape is gone. One question though."

"Which is?"

"This man was a rough character; in and out of jail his entire life. In June '86 he spent a night in the Halifax jail for a drunk and disorderly. He gave his address as Mackerel Point Road a few miles from here off the Peggy's Cove Road. Ever hear of him?"

Beth caught her breath. "Detective I did not know the man who was murdered in my bar. I was in Toronto then. Is that all?"

The detective saw Beth's anxiety. He had not expected such a reaction from her.

"I requested the scene be cleaned. Are you feeling okay? You're suddenly quite pale."

"I'm fine. Just haven't been getting much sleep. Thank you for the information Detective."

Beth hurried past him, past Sal and out the door. Getting into her car, the retching began as soon as she turned the key in the ignition. Anxiety grabbed her gut. She opened the small pillbox she kept in her bag. Popping the medication under her tongue, she eased the car out onto the highway.

Detective Connors watched from his office window as she ran to her car. *Attractive woman,* he thought, *with secrets.*

No. I'm not fine, you asshole! Beth said to herself. The mention of Mackerel Point Road triggered memories of the worst year of her life.

*   *   *

In 1986 Beth Johnston was the brightest girl in her 12th grade class. Popular with her classmates and athletic she was considered by her teachers to be the student most likely to succeed. She dated Jaime Mason, the boy most unlikely to succeed. He took no interest in academics; he preferred rebuilding motorcycles.

Beth and Jaime met in the summer of 1985.

Dave Johnston, Beth's father read the notice Jaime posted on the community bulletin board. Jaime was offering his summer vacation to work on old motorcycles. After opening *Pat Murphy's* Dave stored his 1970 Harley Davidson. Following a discussion with Jaime, Dave hired him to restore the bike.

Beth accompanied her father when the Harley was delivered to Mackerel Point. She was impressed with the conversation Dave and Jaime had and saw a different side of her father. Expressing an interest to learn, Beth asked for permission to return.

And so Beth's free time from her duties at *Pat Murphy's* was spent perched on a stool in that garage. Jaime enjoyed her company and the opportunity to share his knowledge. She encouraged him in his work as no one else ever had. They fell in love.

In early September the Harley was ready for the road. Beth drove Dave to Mackerel Point one morning for a test drive. When he saw Jaime greet his daughter, Dave was alarmed by their obvious romantic relationship.

The bike started immediately. Dave waved, dropped into gear and headed for home to talk to his wife.

Lennie, Beth's mother grinned as her husband parked the Harley at their back door. "Brings back memories Dave. Enjoy the ride?"

"Never mind that. Are you aware of what's going on with Beth and that kid?"

"Yes, our daughter has a crush on Jaime. I suppose the Pub has been to busy for you to notice. Don't worry Dave. All girls her age have summer loves. When school starts up, Beth will get over it. You'll see."

Instead as summer turned to fall the relationship blossomed. Beth and Jaime were inseparable; after school sitting at the Johnston's kitchen table doing homework and on weekends together in the garage warmed by an old pot bellied stove.

Christmas came and went. Beth's grades continued to be outstanding and Jaime found he was able to do school work after all. He was convinced, as was Beth that he would graduate in June. He made application to trade school early in 1986 and was accepted into a Mechanic Program pending his final grades.

All of that changed in April of 1986. Jaime's Uncle Leon came to visit Mackerel Point. In one afternoon he destroyed the hopes and dreams of Beth Johnston and Jaime Mason.

While Beth survived the horror, her life abruptly took an entirely different direction.

A manda Stewart was packing.

Her flight was scheduled to depart in three hours. She'd enjoyed the brief conversation earlier with the bartender, Beth and decided the woman was quite pretty. No time to get to know her better, not now. Satisfied with her performance at the police interview about Leon's death, she felt elated. They had no idea who he was.

"I'm shocked that man died." She had said. "I spoke to him briefly, you know, to be polite. He was really drunk. I find drunks repulsive. I didn't even finish my beer and left. Crowded bars are not my style. Why am I here? I write for a travel magazine. Doing a piece on Peggy's Cove in the winter. Here's my card, Alison McLaughlin. My picture is on it so you will remember me. You can reach me by cell phone or through the agency if need be. I have a flight home to Toronto in a few hours. Is that a problem?" *Take that Ali, serves you right for not answering my e-mail.* The handsome Detective Connors told her he would be in touch.

A reporter approaching her as she left the building was a gift. She gave him Alison's name, then told him she could not talk about the events of the night.

Back at the Inn she thought, *Mexico here I come.* Piling her bags into the back of the rental car she prayed the roads were clear. The wind was still howling, blowing the dusting of snow into peaked drifts.

The storm calmed, the Stanfield airport was operational. Amanda boarded the flight to Cancun. Winter was simply much better in the south. Come summer, she planned to be in the south of France. And she was free.

I am so glad I adopted rich.

Calming herself she settled into the leather seat of Executive Class; she kicked off her boots and leaned back. Five hours to review the events of the past year, the past two days, and to update her journal. The journal her therapist suggested would help her sort through the feelings at the root of her meaningless existence. Of course Dr. Marriott hadn't used those words but Amanda read between the lines. The court made being followed by a therapist a condition of the reduced driving charge thus enabling her to travel internationally.

After a stint in rehab this time last year Amanda decided to track down the culprits responsible for her birth. Her 'parents' were so pleased to have her sober they rewarded her by throwing more money her way. They obviously weren't listening to the scores of counselors who tried their best to discourage such rewards.

Hiring a Private Investigator in Vancouver was a breeze, with her ability to pay an obscene retainer. "Whatever you need to do, find them", she instructed him.

When he did, Amanda finally understood, and the rush of emotion made her craving for booze fill every cell of her body. But the countless hours of lectures had convinced her that messed up on drugs and booze she could not achieve her goals in life.

Her journal entry of August 7th 2010 read,

> *My mother was raped; she lives in Nova Scotia. My father is a rapist; he is in prison. I was born in Toronto. I have a sister and a half brother.*

Amanda became obsessed with orchestrating a meeting of her biological family. She knew she needed to set the stage precisely. She required more information.

Later in August 2010 she wrote,

> *My sister's name is Alison. From the pictures we are obviously identical twins though she has no sense of style. She got artists for parents. Apparently Alison McLaughlin is an up and coming photojournalist in Toronto.*

Amanda made a trip to Toronto and followed Ali, eventually impersonating her. She breezed into Alison's agency one morning. Smiling and nodding to the receptionist, she searched the cards displayed on the front desk. She picked up one of each, including Alison's.

"Need something Ali? Thought you were off to Collingwood today."

"I am. Just forgot some cards."

The thrill of pulling off the impersonation was better than any hit of cocaine she had ever done.

September 2010 her journal entry read,

> *My brother lives in Halifax. Married with a kid.*
> *Works as a land developer. No idea where his mother is.*
> *My mother owns a pub in Indian Harbour. My old man is*
> *in Dorchester.*

A lison McLaughlin was having trouble focusing.

Waking Thursday morning she experienced a sensation of overwhelming dread. Having landed in Mexico City just before midnight she regretted her decision not to take an earlier flight from Toronto. The overnight bus ride to the West coast had been unpleasant. Broken sleep and the nightmare made rest impossible.

Checking into her room, a shower and strong coffee did not help to clear the fog in her head. When she arrived at the photo shoot she knew the day was not going to go well. As a free lance photographer the ability to pull herself together was her forte. But she was in trouble today.

The morning light was essential for the success of this contract. The weight of the camera around her neck was irritating. She was to photograph surfers on the beach at Sayulita on the Pacific Coast of Mexico. The waves were breaking well and the water was peppered with boards and competitors in brightly colored wetsuits. Crouching at the water's edge she got the perspective planned.

As the morning progressed the beach filled with spectators. Children laughed and played in the shallows. Pausing to watch, suddenly the memory of her recurring nightmare flashed back accompanied by an ominous feeling. Always in the dream, she was standing in what seemed to be a gas station, with girl on her left. She frantically called to the girl but her face was turned away and she did not answer. Ali thought she knew the meaning of the dream. Adopted as an infant, she was convinced she had a sibling. Her parents forbid her any attempt to trace her origin. Out of respect for them she decided not knowing was preferable to hurting them. She knew she was well loved.

A shrill whistle blew, bringing her back to the task at hand. Shaking her head Ali did her best to image the action out on the water. This work would not be her best but would pay the bills. The story was a formula travel piece, action photos, beach shots and a short narrative.

By noon the hot sun was bright overhead. She made her way back to her room at *Les Delphines* and a cold beer. While her work was downloading to the laptop, she dove into the pool. Floating in the cooler water, staring up at the clear blue sky, the silence surrounding her, she started to relax. She could go home tomorrow.

*   *   *

Ali finally landed at Pearson International on Friday night. She left her condo, located in the refurbished Candy Factory on Queen Street East, the Tuesday before. Those few days felt like a few months. Dropping her keys on the hall table she went to the kitchen, opened a bottle of cabernet, poured a generous glass and picking up her camera bag, headed to the computer.

She planned to start the download of her photos, check her e-mail and phone messages then head off to bed. Tomorrow she would do the processing, write the article and drop her work at the office.

The hum of the download began.

Opening her e-mail she saw that the inbox was full. She scanned the senders. Half way down the first page one e-mail stood out. Several weeks ago she had deleted another from the same sender, Amanda Stewart, considering it to be some sort of spam.

The subject line this time read,

Too bad you missed your family reunion.

The feeling she experienced after waking from her nightmare washed over her. The body of the e-mail read,

I was disappointed not to have met you Alison. And now our father is dead. You can expect a call from Detective Connors, RCMP from Tantallon, Nova Scotia.

Ali began to retch. Always when she became anxious her body reacted in that manner. Searching her cosmetic bag, she found her pills. Trying her best to calm down, she fought to avoid the panic attack looming over her.

"This must be a cruel prank." She said out loud. "I'll report it. I'm okay."

As the medication took effect, she thought, *I'll find who this Amanda Stewart is.*

She pulled up a search page and typed in the name. As an after thought, she added her name. Never could she have imagined the real life nightmare she was about to enter.

The search results took her off guard. Topping the list was a reference to her,

Alison McLaughlin, Photojournalist Declines Interview

Ali's head started to spin. *Interview? What interview? What's going on?* Taking a deep breath, she clicked on the link.

Staring back at her was her own image nestled into an article in the Halifax Herald reporting on a murder in Indian Harbour. The reporter wrote that she was one of the visitors present the night a man was murdered in a local pub and when approached she declined interview. *My God! How is this possible? I was in Mexico!*

Returning to the search results, she scanned down. Ignoring further references to her, she selected the first result for Amanda Stewart. Finishing the wine in her glass, she watched as the article loaded.

Amanda Stewart, daughter of shipping magnate Lionel Stewart of Vancouver, BC was charged with Dangerous Driving, a Criminal Offense, the conviction of which

> *results in a Criminal Record, heavy fine and suspension*
> *of license. The family's lawyer Maxwell Weatherby argued*
> *the case before Justice Bryant. The charge was reduced to*
> *Careless Driving.*

Ali stopped reading and pushed her chair back. Was this the woman she was looking for? At two in the morning she would spend the night on this. Her pills had done their job to calm her.

Get organized. Get information. Get help.

Despite the fact she knew better than to mix pills and booze, she laughed out loud. "I need more wine."

Back at the computer, she changed the search to show images. The screen began to fill with pictures of women. She saw herself, the photo taken at the agency for her business card. Focusing only on names, her eyes rose to the picture above each 'Amanda Stewart'. The first two rows, nothing. Second picture, third row was a distant group shot taken onboard a yacht. Enlarging the image, the accompanying article appeared.

Stewart Entertains Dignitaries read the title. Ali didn't bother with the text. She was looking for photos. Scrolling down she saw what she was looking for, a tighter shot. The dreadful nightmare feeling descended accompanied for the first time with a sense of recognition.

"I knew it! I do have a sister, an identical twin sister!" Ali said out loud to the empty room. Within seconds she realized like a frightening child's story, her sister may well be the quintessential evil twin of fairy tales.

She knows who I am. What is she trying to do to me?

Ali's common sense kicked in. *I need to talk to this Detective Connors sooner than later.*

Exhausted and more than a little drunk, Ali found her bed.

A dam Reynoldz bent over the drawings on his desk. The final design for the project was nearing completion. His proposal for a truly green community was accepted by the council six months previously. He felt elated at the time, now was concerned that the costs may be prohibitive to moving forward. Spring, two months away, was the anticipated time to break ground. A nagging headache plagued him day and night. His wife, Jenna complained that he tossed and turned, calling out in his sleep.

'Stress' he kept telling her. But he knew the true origin of his anxiety. Two weeks ago he received a disturbing e-mail from Amanda Stewart, a woman he did not know.

She wrote,

> *You don't know me. But we are family. Curious? I will be staying at the Harbour Inn, Indian Harbour. Meet me in the lounge at six-thirty Wednesday night, March 16. Will explain then. Then we'll go have a drink at Pat Murphy's Pub.*

He had sent a reply asking for an explanation. No answer was forthcoming.

Of course he was curious. Was this a communication from the mother who abandoned him as an infant? Impossible. Those things were not done that way. His parents had been very honest with him about what they knew of his birth. He was born in Halifax to a young woman unable to care for him after three months. After his adoption she and her family left the province. Never was he interested in finding her. Though when his daughter, Sylvie was born he prayed that she would be well. He now wondered if there was some genetic link to the child's developmental delay and her difficult temperament.

And so he lied to Jenna, telling her he needed to go to the Oceanstone for a meeting early Thursday the 17th of March. With the weather unpredictable, he planned to stay at the nearby Harbour Inn on Wednesday night and return home after the meeting. Fraught with guilt, he'd slept poorly since. Nightmares plagued him.

Jenna decided that the couple needed a couple of days to themselves. Adam was to meet with the building committee at the Oceanstone Thursday morning.

"I'm coming with you tomorrow Adam." She said at dinner on Tuesday night. "Mom and Dad said they would love to have Sylvie for a couple of days."

"That is not a great idea. I won't have time for you. I will be home on Thursday anyway. The weather will be lousy. What would you do all day?" Adam was horrified.

"The meeting won't last all day, will it? Being snuggled into a cozy Inn with a good book for a day sounds good to me. And that quaint Pub is there; great food I've heard. I'm coming Adam and that's that." Jenna was not about to take no for an answer. "We can stay another day and just hang out like we used to do."

Adam and Jenna checked into the Harbour Inn Wednesday afternoon. Adam was anxious. Jenna thought he was worried about the meeting.

"It will be fine Adam. You have done a good job. Stop worrying!" she encouraged him as they dropped their bags in the room. "Despite the weather we'll have a nice dinner tonight at Pat Murphy's and look forward to doing nothing tomorrow after your meeting. We can even sleep in on Friday; check out this four-poster!" She bounced on the bed.

Adam had never lied to his wife. He was to meet Amanda in the Inn's lounge before dinner. "Jenna, I need to tell you something. Just listen, okay?"

Adam poured out his heart, the entire content of Amanda's e-mail, his fears and most of all his need to know the real truth about from where he came.

"Jenna, I need to know if my genetics affected Sylvie. This woman might have some answers. Jenna? Jenna?" Despite his size, Adam looked like a little boy.

"Adam, I need a moment." Jenna stormed to the bathroom and slammed the door.

Adam checked his watch, six o'clock. He was to meet Amanda in thirty minutes. Would Jenna come with him?

"Jenna, I don't want to do this alone." Adam put his ear to the bathroom door. He could hear her sobbing. He waited. "Jenna?"

The door opened. "Fine, let's hear what she has to say. We will talk later." Jenna took his hand, "Let's be early."

Amanda was on time. Strutting confidently into the lounge, she extended her hand to Adam. She wasn't expecting Jenna to be there.

"I'm Amanda. Adam?" she cooed. "And this must be your lovely wife, Jenna."

Amanda looked into Jenna's eyes with a piercingly cold acknowledgment and with the unspoken message, *Don't mess with me.*

Jenna got the message loud and clear. Ignoring the implicit warning, she stood and extended her hand. "Interesting to meet you Amanda. Adam told me about your mysterious e-mail. Shall we all sit?"

Impressive, Amanda thought. Not many women ever stood up to her. Jenna's handshake was much firmer than Adam's.

"Indeed, let's do that."

B ruce Matthews was beyond disappointed.
On the evening of March 16, ordering a round for the house at *Pat Murphy's* did not have the result he anticipated. Despite his receding hairline and graying beard he expected Beth to recognize him. She did not.

* * *

As executor of his mother's estate Bruce discovered the old Mackerel Point property was his only inheritance. Realizing a return to Nova Scotia was necessary, he experienced a rush of mixed emotion. The long hours alone crossing the country from British Columbia prepared him to face the memory of his shattered youthful dreams.

* * *

Raised in a troubled family, the man recalled what his mother told him before she passed away.

His father, Trent found his first love in a liquor bottle. In his teen years, Trent and his older brother, Leon sold marijuana to pay for their booze. When Leon moved to a Halifax apartment on Hollis Street, Trent dropped out of high school to follow him. Well known at the downtown bars, the brothers found profit in their illegal activities. Leon pushed his brother to engage in dealing harder drugs. Trent refused. He'd met and fallen in love with Lil Matthews.

In 1967 Trent returned to St Margaret's Bay. Lil, now his bride of six weeks, arrived with him. Their baby was due in the spring. Finding the house on Mackerel Point Lil looked forward to a safer life without her brother-in-law Leon. Trent stayed sober, appearing content in his role as a husband.

He supported Lil during her labor and delivery and was delighted when the couple brought their son home.

With bills piling up and Trent unable to find work, Lil cut short her maternity leave. She supported the family working as an ICU nurse at the Victoria General Hospital.

Trent thrived as a stay-at-home father, doing odd jobs and working on the lobster boats when he was able.

He renewed his old friendship with Dave Johnston and got involved in the community of Indian Harbour.

In February 1969 two little girls were born. Dave and his wife, Lennie adored their daughter Elizabeth. Trent and Lil named their second child Gina, after her grandmother Mason.

Gina presented the Mason family with challenges from the moment of her birth. She required two days in the hospital's Neonatal Unit to monitor her respiration. The baby's breathing settled. Lil had planned to nurse her child. But Gina sputtered and choked at the breast, leaving her mother frustrated and her father terrified. Bottle-feeding was simply easier. At home Gina became the center of attention. She fussed and cried far more than her brother had as a newborn. Lil's mood declined. Her two-year old son demanded her attention. Her husband criticized her lack of ability to meet his needs. Lil chose to focus what energy she had entirely on her children.

Trent went to his friend for advice. Dave said physical activity was his way of coping and asked Trent to help renovate the old two-storey building on the wharf. By the holiday weekend in May the work was complete. Dave opened the doors to *Pat Murphy's Pub* on the ground floor overlooking the harbour. Trent drank the first draught beer tapped from the keg.

As the years slipped by Trent spent increasingly less time with his wife and children. Having convinced Dave to buy a pool table for the pub, Trent passed most of his waking hours perfecting his game. Hustling visitors put money in his pocket and supplied his drink.

*   *   *

In April of '86 Trent's older brother showed up in the Bay. Leon strolled into *Pat Murphy's* on a sunny Saturday afternoon. As usual, Trent was winning beer at the pool table. Dave Johnston never forgot the moment the Mason brothers reunited.

"Four ball cross side, don't scratch!" Leon whispered in his brother's ear.

Trent stood back, grabbed his brother and with a roaring laugh, threw him to the floor.

From his position in the dust Leon called out, "Dave, a round for the house. Trent boy, you missed me eh? Now go make the shot!"

That night Lil collected her husband and her brother-in-law after pub closed. Home in Mackerel Point the brothers sat down at the kitchen table.

"Trent, you're drunk. Go to bed. Leon you sleep on the pullout in the living room." Lil knew her words fell on deaf ears.

Trent stumbled to the cabinet below the sink. Rummaging behind the cleaning supplies, he pulled out a bottle of black rum and set it down on the table.

"Where's my son? Tell him to come have a drink with his father and his Uncle Leon!"

"You leave him alone. He worked late." Lil's instinct told her trouble was brewing. But her worry was not for her son. Having known Leon in Halifax years before, she feared for Gina. With his predilection for young women, Leon was not above trying to have his way with a naive girl such as Gina. Family meant nothing to him.

*   *   *

Bruce Matthews, then known as Jaime Mason, was revolted by what he saw happening in the garage the following afternoon.

Saying nothing to anyone, with only the clothes on his back, he ran. Hitch hiking across the country, he stopped at hostels along the way and eventually landed at a homeless shelter in Vancouver. There he met Father Mark. The priest listened to him, comforted him and gave him hope.

One morning the young man raised his head, walked to the docks and got a job.

In June of '87 he contacted his mother. Lil was overjoyed with his invitation for her and Gina to come live with him in British Columbia. Before agreeing to the move she decided she must tell her son about the day he left home.

*   *   *

Lil found Gina sobbing, curled in the upstairs shower. All Gina said, pointing to her genitals was *Hurt.*

In a rage, Lil stormed into the kitchen, picked up the phone and started to dial. Trent and Leon sat at the table, a bottle of rum half empty before them. Trent grabbed the phone from her hand.

"What's got you so worked up?" Trent pushed her to the wall.

"That animal, your beloved brother, raped your daughter! I am calling the cops."

"Trent shut her up!" Leon stood. For the first time, Trent raised his hand to his wife. Before he delivered the blow Lil screamed, "Get out! Get out now! Or I swear you will have to kill me to shut me up. The two of you, leave now and never come back!"

Leon laughed as he picked up the bottle. "You always were a feisty broad Lilly!" Motioning to the door, "Let's go bro. Susie and Leland deserve a visit."

"Gimme a minute. Money in the flour jar." Dumping the contents, Trent scoffed up the bills Lil thought she had hidden. "Go ahead call the cops, you lying bitch." Taking the truck keys, he followed his brother.

Lil did not make the call. She lived and died regretting not having done so.

Much later Lil realized her son was gone. His girlfriend, Beth refused to take any calls.

A month later Gina had no menstrual period. Her pregnancy test was positive.

Lil was with Gina for the birth of a healthy baby boy. Though Lil contacted an adoption lawyer in her daughter's third trimester, Gina insisted she keep her baby.

"Ma," Gina said quietly, nursing her son. "No man will want me so I'll never have another chance to have a baby. His name is Adam, like in the Bible. Please Ma, let me keep him."

Gazing into the tiny face, Lil was swept up in the joy of a new life. While she feared that Gina could not meet the demands of a newborn, she agreed they would take Adam home.

Three months later Lil called the adoption lawyer again. After the first night shift on her new work schedule, she came home to find Adam screaming in his crib. His diaper had not been changed; the room reeked of feces and vomit. Gina was asleep in her bed, a pillow pulled over her ears.

"Gina, wake up!" Lil shook her. Adam quieted in his grandmother's arms. "What were you thinking?"

"The baby kept crying Ma, I didn't know what to do." Gina answered. "I'm sorry Adam. I can't do it; I can't be your mommy."

After giving Adam up for adoption, Gina became withdrawn.

* * *

Jaime did not tell his mother what he saw that day in April '86. Instead he encouraged her to bring his sister to a new life far away from Mackerel Point.

Gina was overwhelmed with big city life. The grief of losing Adam consumed her thoughts. Falling into promiscuity and drug abuse, she died on the day of Adam's first birthday. The police found her body in a Gastown alley. The coroner ruled the cause of death as a heroine overdose.

Both Jaime and his mother changed their names after Gina's death. Lil resumed her maiden name of Matthews; Jaime took Matthews as his surname and his middle name Bruce. He obtained his GED, qualified for admission to the British Columbia Institute of Technology and successfully completed the four-year apprenticeship in Motorcycle Mechanics.

At forty-four, Bruce taught a popular course in Motorcycle Restoration at BCIT. With a specialized shop of his own, he employed the most talented of his students. By all standards he was successful.

On the evening of March 16, 2011 as he watched Beth Johnston serving the customers of Pat Murphy's Pub, he felt the full impact of failure.

L eon Mason grinned as he left Dorchester Penitentiary.
 Ten years in prison had been a waste of time. He had aged. His hair had gone completely gray during the first year of his incarceration. His now full moustache and long white beard altered his former slick appearance to one of an old man. He became known as 'Leon, the Lion'.

His brother Trent visited once a year, but did not appear on the day of his release as promised. On his last visit his little brother looked lousy, skin and bones. Said he had cancer, pancreas. No one else from his past ever visited. But Leon retained good connections to the outside. His cellmate for the last five was brother-in-law to one of his old drug buddies in Halifax.

Last year he began to get letters from some bleeding heart intent on assisting him in his rehabilitation. He wrote back, contrite, welcoming her help. After a couple of months he started to look forward to her biweekly letters. The game he played with her passed the time. He got into her head with his words of thanks for her caring and concern. She fell for it, hook, line and sinker. She sent him her picture, hot looking twenty something redhead.

And the week before his release a bus ticket arrived with a letter outlining a date, place and time to meet her. He laughed when he read the directions to the meeting spot, like he didn't know where Pat Murphy's Pub was!

He was able to use the rehabilitated con with his old landlord in Halifax. He wrote to him, included the letter from his prison counselor saying what a model inmate Leon had been and how he would be able to become a productive member of society. Well, it became a walk in the park.

That same counselor got him a job. A pizza joint at the bottom of Inglis St agreed to take him on as a dishwasher. As if that would satisfy him. But it would not be a bad front for the more lucrative business he knew so well. He knew his old friends from the Blues Bar would be more than happy to see him again. Paying rent would not be a problem.

Arriving in Halifax after an eight-hour train trip from New Brunswick, Leon was within walking distance to his old apartment on Hollis Street. The downtown had changed in ten years. The film studio by the waterfront appeared abandoned, yuppie infested condos had sprung up along the waterfront. *Never mind, the important things are the same,* he thought hefting his bag to his shoulder and navigating his way down the icy sidewalk to the old apartment building.

"Long as you pay the rent and don't cause me no trouble, I'll have ya here. First time you screw up, you're out." The landlord said handing Leon the keys. "Garbage day is Tuesday, mailbox in the hallway and don't mess up the furniture."

"No problem my friend. Got a job. I'm good, you'll see." Leon flashed his very best smile. "Thank you."

Climbing the three flights of stairs to the furnished apartment Leon was intent on dumping his duffle bag, taking a pee and heading to the bar. He would show up at his new job on the weekend. He planned to make a lot more money before then, use his ticket to the Bay and have some fun with his redhead.

The boys were in the bar. He scored, set up a couple of buys and enjoyed the music of the Tuesday night band. Tempted by a few of the young women dancing on the small floor, he restrained himself.

Save it for tomorrow night. He grinned at the thought. *When is the last time you had a sweet young redhead!*

*   *   *

The freezing wind continued to blow late Wednesday afternoon as Leon walked along Hollis Street to the Acadian terminal. He took the back seat on the bus headed to St Margaret's Bay.

On the thirty-minute trip he thought about how he would spend the time until he met Ms Amanda Stewart. Her directions suggested he call some guy called Jimmy Moore to drive him out to Indian Harbour from the bus stop at the Crossroads. The hell with that, he'd hitch a ride; save the money for a beer or two. He would drop in on the lads down on the docks; see if anyone would put him up for the night.

Traffic heading out the Peggy's Cove road at six in the afternoon was busier than he expected as he got off the bus. Sticking out his thumb, two guys headed to the Oceanstone picked him up. Leon had no recollection of the place but said that was good for him. He sat in the back seat, leaning on the window watching familiar landmarks as they passed. He was surprised when the car pulled over, hell they were in Indian Harbour; close enough to walk to his first destination.

"Thanks for the ride gentlemen. Can I give you a couple of bucks for gas?" Leon opened the door.

"No, no that's not necessary. Do you have far to go? Weather is getting snotty. We don't mind taking you somewhere. No trouble." The driver sounded concerned. Typical Nova Scotian.

"Walking distance, no problem. I'm good. Thanks again." Leon waved as the car turned into the driveway and disappeared from sight. Only then he picked up his steps, anxious to get to the docks. The timing was perfect. With this wind he knew the boats would be on their moorings, and that the crews were checking them.

The boat with which he had been so familiar, *Evie*, a 30-foot Cape Islander was moving with the wind. He saw his brother-in-law jump into one of the tenders tied to the stern.

Leon stood in the center of the driveway from the dock to the highway, bent over, hands on his knees. The truck stopped before him.

"What the hell buddy?" The driver leaned out the window.

Leon raised his head to look into the eyes of his brother in law. "Hey Leland, how's my sister?"

"You son of a bitch! What the hell are you doing here? I should run you over right now! Get outta my way." Leland revved the truck's engine. Leon heard the shift into first gear. He rolled onto the ground as the pickup squealed away.

"You're still the same asshole." Leon laughed out loud. He picked himself up and headed up to the dock. The wind was strong and chilling. The crews were making their way ashore. No one recognized Leon nor did they pay any attention to him as he lit up a joint. He hoped to interest one of them in a buy. He hung around awhile.

"No takers?" he offered. "Got some good weed here guys." The boys were more interested in feeling the warmth of the pub.

Leon followed them up the hill to Pat Murphy's. He could use a cold beer. He wondered if Dave still owned the pub.

The place smelled the same; old wood and stale beer. He was sorry to see that the pool table was gone, replaced with painted tables. He remembered the place being larger. A big screen television was showing the weather channel. The guys were gathered at the bar. Leon took his place in the line to get a beer. As he waited some guy hollered out, "A round of Keith's draught for the house." Knowing their beer would be delivered to them, a roar went up as the crowd at the bar dispersed to gather at tables surrounding the television.

A seat at the end of the bar opened up. Leon sat there. Beth Johnston, without a glance at him, set a full glass of beer on the bar in front of him. He knew her instantly. She was as luscious today as she was as a teenager.

The heavy door to the pub opened. And in came the redhead. As she approached him, tossing her ponytail, Leon found himself more excited than he'd imagined.

L eland Boutilier struggled to make a living.

He knew he was a loser. And his nagging wife reminded him daily that was the case. They certainly hadn't married for love. In 1966 while the rest of the world enjoyed a fresh outlook on life, the old rules stood in rural Nova Scotia. Back seat sex on grad night resulting in a baby meant a wedding.

Regardless, Leland was enthralled with his baby daughter, Brandy. He was determined to give her and Susan a good life and to be a better father and husband than his old man was.

He refused to work on his father's boat in the beginning. He chose to take a job as a labourer with the government on road crews. The money was good and he came home on Friday night with no worries. When his first son, Danny came along Leland had visions of he and his son in business together building houses. He was happy.

But when his father had a stroke and was no longer able to manage his boat, Leland believed he had no choice in his destiny. The lobster license must stay in the family. So Leland took over the operation of *Evie* with his two younger brothers as crew. As the years passed Leland became increasingly bitter as he watched his old friends leave West Dover for the promise of big money out west. He started drinking heavily and picking fights.

In 1986 after all the trouble with Susan's brothers, Trent and Leon, his daughter Brandy left home. At nineteen the girl was a popular vocalist with local bands. With an offer to become a member of a blues group in Halifax she was glad to leave West Dover. The band had steady gigs at several bars so she made a decent living. She saw her parents on holidays, her brothers came to town often to watch her perform. Then in 1999 her Uncle Leon showed up in the crowd. Try as she might to ignore him, he cornered her by the washrooms during a break. She was disgusted and afraid as he tried to paw her, the way he had when she was younger. Breaking away from him she headed straight to the bouncer on duty and had Leon thrown out. But Leon hung around outside peddling dope. He was careful following her and her friends as they walked home. When a knock came on her door Brandy thought it was a friend needing a place to stay so she opened the door. Leon pushed the door wide. His purpose was clear.

Leland and Susie supported their daughter through the horror of the rape trial. After Leon was sentenced and was being led out of the courtroom, Leland screamed "I'll kill you when you get out."

INVESTIGATION

Detective Connors read the coroner's final report of Leon Mason's murder. Cause of death was a collapsed lung resulting from a single stab wound to the left side of the chest. Forensics had little to add. The toxicology screen came back positive for cannabis, cocaine and a significant amount of sedative. The weapon removed at autopsy was an old ice pick. No useable fingerprint was found. The transcripts of the thirty-three video interviews were no more helpful to him than on the night of the crime. Witnesses confirmed that a man was sleeping hunched over the bar of Pat Murphy's Pub on the stormy Wednesday that closed down fishing.

He reviewed Leon Mason's criminal record. He interviewed the prison staff. By all accounts Leon had caused no trouble.

The information he was able to get from Leon's dealer connections in Halifax provided no leads. Leon disappeared and died before his deals went through.

The uncomfortable impression Beth Johnston left with him when they last met still nagged at him. Was there a link between her and the victim?

He confirmed Beth's statement that she was in Toronto in 1986. She left Nova Scotia early that summer. She stayed with her mother's sister, Moriah, who told him that Beth had been hoping to attend Ryerson. Unfortunately she missed the fall admission date. Beth waited tables in a downtown bar in hopes of admission the next year. In February of 1987 Dave, Beth's father suffered a heart attack. Beth returned to Nova Scotia. At eighteen she took over managing Pat Murphy's Pub. Dave died in April and Lennie, Beth's mother passed away from cancer the following year.

Beth was a respected member of her community. She contributed to the growth and prosperity of Indian Harbour. And when Detective Connors was honest with himself, he found he was very attracted to her.

Detective Eli Connors, at forty-five was an eligible bachelor. Or at least, so people told him. When he looked at himself in the mirror, which he rarely did, he saw a short, dumpy, almost middle-aged cop. Raised in Ingonish, Cape Breton, all Eli wanted for his life was to be a member of the RCMP. Rising to Detective status last year, fulfilled his childhood dream.

He consciously never entered into a longstanding relationship, though he had not been without female companionship. His father had been an example to him.

"A cop's life means the job comes first." His dad said to Eli on the day of his graduation. "Your mother left me because I lived by that."

He often wondered if his life now would be fuller had he allowed himself to fall in love. His days began and ended in the gym. In between times he was immersed in the cases he was investigating. He had few friends and fewer outside interests.

The Leon Mason case consumed him. He was waiting for results on the make of the murder weapon. The ice pick was an antique, he was sure of that. His own research had given him an expanded appreciation for the murder weapon. Ice picks had a variety of uses including ice sculpting, leather punch, and mechanic's tool; an all round useful object.

Going back through the interviews he created a short list for further questioning; Alison McLaughlin, Adam and Jenna Reynoldz, Bruce Matthews, Beth Johnston, Jimmy Moore and Leland Boutilier. Recalling faces was a talent Eli was proud of and found to be extremely valuable, as was the ability to catch innuendos of expression in conversation. He started with Alison McLaughlin.

A tall, svelte young woman of twenty-four, Alison had attitude. Her chin length auburn hair framed an attractive face but her eyes, a deep navy blue, were cold. He was surprised when he compared his memory to the image on her business card. He saw the same facial features, however the smile and the eyes were very different from the person he met. He dialed the cell phone number.

This is Alison. I am unable to take your call. Please leave a message.

"Detective Connors calling. Please return the call at 902-555-4252 as soon as possible."

Different quality to the voice, one that had a hint of anxiety Eli thought.

Moving on, he dialed the Halifax number that Adam Reynoldz gave him.

"*Come By Soon Antiques and Collectibles*, can I help you?" A woman answered.

"Am I speaking to Jenna Reynoldz?" Eli scribbled 'antiques' by her name.

Hesitation, "This is Jenna. Who's speaking?" Not so friendly now, Eli noted.

"Detective Connors here Mrs. Reynoldz. Some additional information has come to my attention. Is it possible for you and your husband to meet with Detective Rutherford and me tomorrow afternoon? We could come by at 3 o'clock." Eli waited.

"Oh yes, Detective Connors, I do recognize your voice. What information? We told you all we knew that night."

"Just need to ask you both a couple of questions to finish my report. Shouldn't take more than half an hour. I would really appreciate your time Jenna."

"Well, I guess that would be okay. Adam is working at home these days and as you now realize, I have a small business here."

"Thank you, I'll see you tomorrow." Eli continued his notes as he hung up the receiver.

He pictured the couple. Jenna, a petite brunette came to the detachment on the night of the murder, visibly shaken. Adam, towering over her by at least a foot, was stony faced and remained as such throughout the interview. At the time Eli read the discrepancy as individual shock reactions. Now he was not so sure.

His line rang. "Yes Sal?"

"Incoming call for you, line two, Alison McLaughlin returning your call."

"Thanks, put her through."

Quick reply. This is good, he thought.

"Hello, Ms McLaughlin?"

"Yes, call me Ali. I am so glad you called. There has been a horrible mistake. I've been up all night trying to make sense of it all." Ali took a breath.

"Slow down Ms McLaughlin, go easy. Where are you?" Eli motioned Sal to pickup.

"I'm home, in my apartment in Toronto. I thought about getting on a plane to Halifax this morning but was just too tired. But I booked for tomorrow if the weather stays clear. I need help Detective Connors. The more I find out, the more afraid I am."

"Has someone threatened you?"

"Not directly, I don't think anyway. But a woman named Amanda Stewart appears to be impersonating me." Ali's speech was not as pressured. "Can I make an appointment to see you? My flight arrives in the morning."

"I could pick you up and drive you into the city."

"That would be so helpful. Detective Connors I have never been to Halifax, is the airport very big? I'm coming in on the Air Canada flight arriving at eight."

"No, the airport is very small compared to Pearson. I will be waiting at the arrival gate."

"I am not used to feeling this way. I am usually quite together." She laughed. "I have a lot to tell you."

"Tomorrow then, Stanfield Airport 8am; I'll be there." Eli heard the dial tone and hung up. *That is not the woman who was in Pat Murphy's Pub. What next?*

Eli left his office, poured himself a coffee from the continually brewing pot in the staff lounge and collapsed in one of the soft chairs. Sal was hot on his heels.

"So, that was interesting!" Intrigue was not a usual part of Cpl Sal Walters day.

"Will I get to meet her?"

"Cpl Walters I needed you to listen in because you are the only other person here. And you were here the night of the murder. You met Alison McLaughlin. Did that sound like the woman you met?"

"That was not the woman I met Detective Connors. The woman I met sat in the waiting room like she owned the place. Kept looking at her watch and telling me every five minutes that she had a plane to catch. If it is the same woman, we're talking Jekyll & Hyde!"

"Exactly. And yes, I expect you will meet her." Eli emptied his cup. "Two more calls to make. Do something for me. Call Jimmy Moore and Leland Boutilier and make appointments for them to come in to see me on Monday? One in the morning and one in the afternoon."

"Sure. I'll leave a note for you on the times in your mailbox Almost end of shift for me." Sal grinned. "Saturday night date waiting for me. No need to ask what you're doing!"

Eli shot her his very best dirty look, walked back to his office and closed his door. Bruce Matthews was his next call. Intentionally he was leaving Beth until last. As he expected, dialing Bruce's number sent him directly to a message.

"You have reached Bruce at Matthews Motorcycle Repair & Restoration. Leave a message."

"Detective Connors speaking. You indicated that you would be in Nova Scotia for ten days. Some additional information has come to my attention regarding the matter of Pat Murphy's Pub. Please return my call to set up a further interview. 902-555-4252."

Eli was aware that Bruce had driven across the country in preference to flying. At the time of his initial meeting he thought that was odd, considering the time of year. Bruce told him the trip was a business write off by driving, stopping along the way at various shops and suppliers. Eli had accepted that as plausible. Given the today's bizarre conversations, perhaps there was another very good reason.

Eli stared at the file containing the interviews with Beth Johnston. This was not a call he was in a hurry to make. Should he leave a message on her home phone, call her cell or call the Pub? Saturday night would be busy at Pat Murphy's.

Never, never, never mix business with your personal life! His father's warning resounded in his mind. *What the hell, a guy has to eat! I'll make it a social call and set up an appointment.*

Eli shut down his computer, forwarded his personal line to his cell, picked up the note from Sal, grabbed his jacket and headed out to Pat Murphy's Pub. The roads were clear and the forecast was for sunny skies over the next couple of days. The twenty-kilometer drive to Indian Harbour was interrupted by a call on his cell phone. Pulling over into the parking lot at Paul's Hall, he answered.

"Detective Connors speaking."

"Hello Detective, Bruce Matthews returning your call."

"Mr. Matthews, thanks for getting back to me so soon. Are you still in the area?"

"I am, probably for another week. As I mentioned to you I am trying to settle my mother's estate. It is taking longer than I expected."

"Not surprising. Are you still staying at the Harbour Inn? As I said in my message, I got some information and I wanted to set up a time for us to meet."

"Ah, I have been sleeping at the Inn. I'm in Halifax now just tying up some business. I can be available on Monday or Tuesday next week."

"Tuesday is best. Let's say ten that morning."

"That is good with me." Bruce hesitated. "Can you tell me if the pub is open? I never did get to speak with Beth Johnston."

"I assume the pub is open. The investigators have finished there. As a matter of fact I am on my way there for dinner."

Bruce felt foolish. He worried that the detective would misinterpret his concern. "Please give Beth my best."

Well, well, that was interesting. Eli thought as he ended the call.

The light was on at Pat Murphy's Pub when he pulled in, though there were only two cars in the parking lot. He had expected to see it full. He realized why when he read the notice tacked on the wall below the bell.

CLOSED UNTIL MONDAY
Free bowl of Marg's Chowder 5 to 7 pm.
Thanks, Beth.

Eli rang the brass bell anyway. Beth opened the door a crack with the intention of pointing to the sign saying the pub was closed. When she saw Eli she pushed the door open wide.

"Detective Connors, this is a surprise! Come in."

Eli felt awkward. Beth was radiant in the soft light. Her long, auburn hair was pulled back into a ponytail with wisps free around her face. Wearing a bright lime green turtle neck under a pair of loose overalls she looked comfortable, relaxed and to him, very feminine. He nodded and stepped inside.

"I should have called." Eli said.

"Oh, that's alright. Marg and I have spent the past couple of days tidying up. I know you told me the place had been cleaned, but I had to do it for myself. And I had Jeff, the carpenter who helps me come in and we redesigned the bar. You can understand why." Beth did not appear anxious in the least.

The pub was small and L-shaped. The total floor space was not more than 900 square feet. Jeff had cut away the end of the bar connected to the wall where Leon sat the night he was murdered. Beth now had the ability to move around the bar. Only three stools would sit before her.

"Good job. Much better flow." Eli commented.

"And we've rearranged the tables by the stairs up to the Grille. In fact we moved a couple of them upstairs so people could have a little more privacy away from the noise on busy nights, keep Marg company and make more room down here for her to move around." Beth was obviously more than okay. "So why are you here?"

"Beth, the place looks wonderful." Eli ignored the hunger rumblings in his belly. "I do need to talk to you more about Wednesday night. I live out this way on Paul's Point so I decided to drop out to set up another interview."

Marg came down the stairs. "I heard you say you are Detective Connors so I assume you are here on business." She extended her hand to Eli. "Marg Snair. I'm finished here for the night. '*Too pooped to pop.*' as my dad used to say. Call me tomorrow Beth. We will have a great reopening Monday!" Marg breezed out the door leaving Eli and Beth alone.

The mood abruptly changed.

"Another interview? I'm not going to like that one any better than the first, am I Detective Connors?"

Eli fought the urge to say *Call me Eli.* Instead he replied, "Perhaps not Beth, but it is necessary."

"Just get Sal to call with a day and time. I will cope. However, I'm pleased you dropped by tonight. I have something to say to you and I'd rather do it here." Beth pulled out a chair. "Have a seat. Do you have a first name? Or am I being too familiar? I'm afraid all I can offer as a beverage is beer or a pop."

Eli rationalized the situation in seconds. *She cannot be the murderer. I'm off duty. She agreed to an interview.* He thought while he considered his options. *She is just so gorgeous!*

"I'll have a Keith's. And my name is Eli."

Beth set down two bottles of Keith's on the table and sat across from him. "Salute!" she said as she clinked his bottle with hers.

"Eli, I misled you. I did recognize the man who was murdered here. When I was seventeen that man raped me. But I saw his face only briefly at that time." Beth's demeanor was aloof, as if she was talking about someone else. Yet she was unable to look directly at Eli. "That day my life changed and the lives of the people I loved." She took a drink.

Eli realized he was making an error in judgment by allowing her to continue. Ignoring the warning resounding in his mind he stayed quiet.

"I was in a serious relationship with Leon's nephew, Jaime. I spent weekend days with him in the garage at his home on Mackerel Point Road. He was a magician with motorcycle rebuilds. He fixed my dad's bike. Jaime and I had big plans for the future."

Beth went on, "But one Saturday in April Leon Mason appeared at Pat Murphy's. I was home doing a school project that day, so I wasn't working. My dad warned me not to go to see Jaime the next day, Sunday. He didn't tell me why. Like a typical teenage girl in love, I ignored his warning and rode my bike over anyway. It was just before lunch. I had packed Jaime's favorite sandwich for a picnic." Beth took a deep breath; her eyes began to tear. "This is the difficult part Eli."

Eli couldn't speak; he was in too deep now.

"I parked my bike by the side of the house and headed to the garage. I could hear a ruckus. I figured Jaime and Gina must be having a disagreement. They often did." Beth paused.

"When I opened the door I saw them. But it wasn't Jaime in the garage. I surprised the man and he stood up, fumbling with his jeans. Gina stopped screaming, got up off the floor and pulled down her skirt. The man had his back to me. Gina ran past me out the door, slamming it closed. I tried to go after her but his hand reached out and grabbed my arm. It felt like a vise. He laughed and said, "Come to Uncle Leon."

"Time changed, I mean I felt like I was in slow motion. He turned my arm behind my back. I tried to call for Jaime but he covered my mouth with his other hand and leaned me over Jaime's workbench. Then I couldn't scream. I tried to move my body away from him. He had a weapon of some sort, began threatening me. I froze. In my head I was screaming to fight, to stop what I knew was about to happen. I was powerless, terrified and angry, very angry. I felt the pain when he . . . he penetrated me but the worst thing was losing my freedom, having no choice, being controlled and used."

"At some point I heard the door open. I turned my head to try and see. That's when I first saw Leon Mason's face." Beth became quiet. "I think it was Jaime that opened the door. I have spent twenty-five years hating him for not helping me. He went away that day and I have never seen or heard from him since."

Beth stood and began to pace. "Finally Leon released his hold. I raced home and told no one what had happened. When my mother saw that I was upset and crying, I told her Jaime and I had quarreled. Dad was at the pub." Beth paused. Her voice began to shake. "I was a virgin. Jaime and I decided we would stay that way until we were married. So I wasn't on any birth control. When I missed my period in May, I tried to put it down to stress, but deep down I knew better."

"I graduated from High School in mid-June, but still I'd had no period. I called my Aunt Moriah in Toronto asking her if I could come to stay with her, making up a story that I was hoping to attend Ryerson. I said nothing about my true situation. When Aunt Moriah called back to accept, my parents were delighted. I would be leaving the Bay to study while staying safe with family."

Beth looked at Eli. "I know this is a lot Eli. And there is more."

Eli wanted to speak but was torn between his position as the lead detective in this murder case and a man perilously close to falling in love with a woman who might be a murderer.

"I was pregnant. I guess that is obvious from what I've told you so far. What's worse, I was pregnant with twins. When I got to Toronto I told Aunt Moriah I was pregnant, swearing her to secrecy. I was not in a position to be a mother, never mind in those circumstances. She kept my secret. My parents never knew they were grandparents. I made a private adoption arrangement in my eighth month. I never saw my babies. I delivered them by C-section and left the hospital three days later. Three weeks after their birth I was so curious about my children that I contacted the lawyer I used. He told me that on their way home the couple was killed in a freak head on collision, waiting to turn into a rest stop to gas up. The babies survived and several weeks later were adopted, but separately. He couldn't give me more information because the documents were sealed." Beth said, a deep sadness on her face, and in her voice.

She sat, looked at him. "So on the night he was murdered, I did recognize Leon Mason. And God help me, I was glad he was dead. But I did not kill him."

*   *   *

Early Sunday morning Eli leaned on the wall across from the Domestic Arrivals door of the Stanfield Airport. He looked up at the flight status board for the fifth time in as many minutes. The Air Canada flight from Toronto had arrived. After his meeting with Beth the night before, he slept poorly and now found himself extremely anxious to meet Alison.

The passengers were coming down the escalator. When he saw the tall redhead wearing a green leather coat, his heart skipped a beat. Watching her he saw Beth as she must have been at twenty-four. She walked through the doors, her eyes connecting to his.

"Detective Connors?" she asked, standing before him.

"Yes. And you are Alison McLaughlin." Eli extended his hand. "Do you have more luggage?"

"No. Just have a carry on. I travel light. Shall we go? How far to Halifax?"

This woman definitely was not the Alison he interviewed after the murder. Physically the two were identical. The energy surrounding this Alison was entirely different.

The drive took thirty minutes. They chatted about nothing in particular on the way. Eli pulled up to the Prince George and parked. Alison opened the door.

"Thank you for coming to the airport for me. I'll check in and drop my bag in the room. Is there somewhere private we can talk? I'm sorry. Do you have somewhere else you need to be?"

"No, but I have a meeting at three. I reserved a private meeting room here for the morning. I'll meet you in the lobby."

Alison smiled Beth's smile. "Perfect! I shouldn't be more than fifteen minutes." She opened the back door to get her bag and walked into the hotel.

Eli took the notebook out of his inside pocket and made a few notes on the page he had titled Alison McLaughlin. He decided his approach today would be simply to take notes as she talked, asking only questions necessary to clarify the content.

Leading the way to the meeting room Eli asked if she wanted coffee or something to eat as they passed the dining room.

"I've had enough coffee over the past forty-eight hours and sufficient red wine!" Alison said. " Had a yogurt on the plane so I'm fine."

"Let me know if you need anything. Here we are." Eli opened the door.

"Oh, this is nice." Alison chose to sit in the first seat to the right of the head of the polished mahogany table. "The head chair is yours." She pulled a file from her bag. Eli took his seat.

"Before we start Alison, do you have any objection to me recording our discussion?"

"Of course not. I expected that. Shall I begin? I tried to come prepared Detective Connors. I brought copies of the e-mails this Amanda Stewart sent to me and the article in your local paper with my picture and saying I declined an interview, which I never did. I brought my passport, copies of my travel and accommodation record for my recent trip to Sayulita. I have a statement from the agency's receptionist who told me I dropped by to pick up some cards last year, which I had not done. Plus I have printed out information about Amanda Stewart that I found doing my research. And I made notes about what I think is happening after quizzing my mother about my biological family." Alison pushed the papers toward him. "I made copies for you. This Amanda person obviously stole my identity."

"Alison, we move a little slower down here in the Maritimes. Thank you for the work you have done but I'll need a bit of time to digest it. Can we just talk for now?" Eli recognized her investigative nature as a defense mechanism.

"Of course, I just thought I might be able to help." Alison's eyes became misty.

"I understand and I do appreciate it. You have had a very unsettling few days."

"I need to know. What happened out there Detective Connors?"

How much can I tell her? Thought Eli. "On the evening of Wednesday, March 16th between the hours of eight to ten pm, a man named Leon Mason was murdered in Pat Murphy's Pub at Indian Harbour. The establishment is small, was crowded and very busy. At closing, the owner of the pub, Elizabeth Johnston discovered the body. The RCMP was called. My fellow detective and I conducted interviews with the patrons of the pub that night."

Eli watched Ali's face. "Among them was a woman who identified herself to us as Alison McLaughlin."

The young woman showed nothing but interest.

Eli continued, "The pub was closed while our Crime Scene crew combed the area and the Coroner compiled her report. When I reviewed the progress on the case, I made a list of the interviews I felt were necessary to repeat. That list, included Alison McLaughlin. I called you, having been given your card by that person. That call brought us to this place, today."

"So, is the other 'Alison McLaughlin', Amanda Stewart a suspect in the murder?" Alison's tears had long dried. She sat forward. "You know that person wasn't me. Is Amanda Stewart trying to frame me? Fascinating. So now what? What can I do?"

"Alison, you've done it. You are here. Amanda is not a suspect in the murder, yet. Nor are you, with the information you brought. There is a case for other charges against her. You might think about that and consult a lawyer." Eli did not say that Amanda now was definitely a person of interest in Leon's murder.

"So was Leon my father? Amanda said our father was dead. What does that mean? What do you think? My mother told me that she and my dad adopted me from an agency in New Brunswick. How do I find out if Amanda was adopted from there too? Is my biological mother alive and if so, where is she?" Despite herself, Alison became emotional.

Eli swallowed hard, trying with all his strength not to show his thoughts on his face, or in his eyes. "Alison, truthfully this case has taken a bizarre turn. When I locate Amanda who seems to be in the thick of this, then I may get the answer to your questions. First I need to find Amanda."

"I know who her parents are and I found their phone number. Well, really the number I found is for the Head Office for Stewart's Shipping in Vancouver. That is all in the papers I brought for you." Alison looked tired.

"Get some rest Alison. Then take a walk around the city. Even at this time of year, you'll find the charm. Expect a call from me Tuesday night. By the way, how long have you planned to stay in Halifax?"

"My return ticket is open. I'm not leaving until I have answers. I want to confront Amanda. She needs to explain her behavior. And since she knows so much . . . I want to find my biological mother!"

Ali smiled Beth's smile again. "I'm used to being on my own Detective Connors. I'm a freelance photojournalist. Surely I can find a piece to write to keep me busy. I will await your call."

*　*　*

Eli and Detective Rutherford turned off the Prospect Road and followed the signs to *Come By Soon Antiques and Collectibles*. At the end of the driveway, the Reynoldz home was nestled in a grove of pines with an outbuilding to the right displaying the shop's sign above the door. He parked by the house. Leaving his car he glanced over at the shop, then stepped up onto the small deck of the main house. The time was precisely three o'clock. Before he could ring Jenna opened the door, inviting them to enter the kitchen.

"Come in gentlemen. Make yourself comfortable. That is a fresh pot of coffee; help yourselves. Mugs, milk and sugar are on the table." She pointed in the direction of the kitchen table.

"I'll just run upstairs to let Adam know you're here."

Eli did pour himself a cup; his partner declined. The coffee was fresh brewed and smelled strong, just as he liked it. He felt the same nostalgia as when he entered his mother's kitchen in Cape Breton. *I'll be damned if a murderer lives in this home,* he thought.

Jenna and Adam came into the kitchen together. Adam offered his hand, "Welcome to our home Detectives. I hope we can be of some assistance."

Adam was relaxed, and appeared genuine in his greeting. "Our daughter, Sylvie is with her grandparents so you have our full attention."

"I'll come straight to the point then. As I understand, you both checked into the Harbour Inn on the afternoon of March 16th, 2011. At your individual interviews with us later that night, each of you gave slightly different stories about why you were in Indian Harbour that night. I expect since then that you have discussed that. So tell me why were you really there that night?"

Jenna's hand lay over Adam's on the table. Eli noted that she increased her grip as Adam began his answer.

"This is about me Detective Connors." Adam began. "Jenna knew nothing about what took me to Indian Harbour that night. In fact, I lied to her until she forced to explain. Let me start at the beginning."

"A very good place to start, and much appreciated Adam." Eli watched the couple's interaction, the lack of eye contact and their body language. He had the unpleasant feeling that no matter what he was about to hear, secrets would continue to be kept from him.

"Several weeks ago I received an e-mail from an Amanda Stewart. Inviting me to meet her upset me very much. I am adopted so when she mentioned family I immediately thought she might be my biological mother looking for me. She did not respond to my questions."

Adam looked at Jenna. "I lied to my wife so that I could meet Amanda. I hadn't been myself lately so Jenna insisted she come with me. Just before meeting I told Jenna the whole story. Thankfully, she agreed to meet Amanda with me."

Adam took a deep breath. "When we met I was in shock, Detective Connors. Jenna can give you better details about the meeting."

"That's fine Adam." Eli decided. "Jenna?"

"As my husband told you, I heard about Amanda Stewart just that evening. Before that I was planning a couple of days away with him alone. The project he is working on has been stressing him. At first I was angry that he lied to me, but I put that aside."

Jenna looked Eli straight in the eye.

"I knew as soon as I saw her that Amanda Stewart was nothing but trouble. She carried on in a melodramatic fashion telling us that an investigator she hired gave her information that Adam's mother was Gina Mason and his father was Leon Mason. Further, Leon was Gina's uncle. She cruelly let Adam realize, if what she said was true, he was a child of incest. We were appalled."

Eli held Jenna's gaze until she looked away. Eli turned to Adam. "Adam, that information must have been very painful for you."

Adam's face paled.

Jenna continued in a harsh voice, "She told us that Leon raped Gina. She told us a family reunion was arranged. Bitch! She said she had invited her sister and their father, also Adam's father, to be at her mother's pub that night, just across the road at Pat Murphy's."

Jenna's face was stony with no emotion. "She enjoyed each revelation and Adam's pain. She smiled as she pointed out that

Adam has two half sisters and at the same time two cousins. But the information she ended with was the most devastating and cruel. When Adam asked if his mother, Gina would be there, that psychopath smirked."

Adam spoke, "She said Gina couldn't come. She killed herself because I was born." He broke down.

Taking charge, Jenna announced, "This interview is over. Leave us alone."

*   *   *

Jimmy Moore was sitting in the waiting room when Eli arrived at the Detachment on Monday morning. "Cpl Walters, please show Mr. Moore to Interrogation."

Eli unlocked his door, hung his jacket over the back of his desk chair and picked up Jimmy's file. He hoped this interview would not add to the complexity of more family history.

"Am I in this here room bein' videoed?"

"Yes Jimmy. Same as the night of the murder, it's the way we do interviews now. I can give you my attention that way. Then I go back and make notes. I can see that makes you anxious."

"Course it makes me nervous. I didn't do nothing wrong."

"This interview is only to help me get some facts clearer in my mind. You are not a suspect Jimmy. I know you were not in the pub at the time of the murder."

"Okay then, just as long as nothing I say will come back to bite me in the ass!" Still Jimmy looked apprehensive.

Eli pushed 'Record' on the desk console.

"Mr. Moore, in your initial interview with Detective Rutherford on the evening of March 16th of this year you stated that you arrived at Pat Murphy's Pub at about ten-fifteen for the purpose of driving Leland Boutilier and his boys to their home. Is that correct?"

"Yes sir. Leland called me on my cell phone at a quarter to ten, just before 'last call'. I was dropping off passengers in Black Point."

"You also told the detective that Beth Johnston asked you for help after your passengers were in your bus."

"That's right. I was about to close the door on that noisy bunch when Beth came out. She looked pissed off and said she needed help. Didn't say why at the time."

"And I understand that Leland Boutilier had been in the front seat and that he got out as well."

"He said he knew Beth would have a time with the customer left at the bar."

Eli made a note. "So the two of you went in to help her?"

"Yeah, but I told Leland to go back to the bus. He was well in the bag. He had his mind made up to come in. In his state I wasn't arguin'. He can be a nasty drunk."

"Did he say anything more?"

"He mumbles when he's loaded. Didn't say much I could understand until he went to go over to the guy. When he got too close Beth told him not to touch anything."

"What did he say then Jimmy?"

Jimmy squirmed in his seat, his face flushing. "I never heard him real clear or nothin' so I likely shouldn't say. Besides, he can be ugly sober too and he's bigger than me."

"What do you think he said Jimmy? Obviously whatever he said might be important. You don't want to be hiding anything from the law do you?"

"No sir." Jimmy took a minute. Eli waited in silence. "Sounded like, 'good riddance ya bastard' and then he stormed out and got back in the bus."

Jimmy was trembling. "You can't tell him I told you that. He'd hurt me for sure. I know I heard the word 'bastard' for sure."

"I understand Jimmy. Did you recognize the victim?"

"No sir. I never got a good look. Got a squeamy stomach. I called the cops like Beth told me to."

"What was the conversation like when you took them all home later on?"

"I was concentrating pretty hard; the wind was blowing hard at Peggy's and that road is twisty to West Dover. We was weavin' all over. Was pretty upsettin' leavin' Beth alone with a dead body." Jimmy paused. "I generally block out drunk talkers. But thinkin' about it now, I get the feeling that them boys knew the guy that died; at least Leland did. Can't recall who said what, but one of them said there was a guy at the dock earlier tryin' to sell dope. I remember Leland said 'Typical'."

"And you didn't tell any of this to Detective Rutherford?"

"No sir, he didn't ask. Besides I just figured Leland was acting smart havin' seen the dead guy up close. The guy musta been a doper. You know, you saw him closer than me."

"Take my card Jimmy. Call me if you recall anything more, or if you hear something you think I should know. And thank you for the information you've given me. You may go now."

Eli returned to his office. Minutes later Cpl. Walters knocked on his door. "Leland Boutilier is here an hour early to see you. He's in a real bad mood. Started cursing at Jimmy as he was leaving. Should I try to get him to Interrogation now or make him wait out by me?"

"Put him in Interrogation to cool off. I need to make a call before I can see him."

Eli dialed the number for Stewart Shipping. British Columbia being four hours behind Nova Scotia, he hoped he could get through to Lionel Stewart directly.

"Stewart Shipping, how may I direct your call?" Eli was amazed to hear the voice of a real person.

"This is RCMP Detective Connors calling from Nova Scotia. I wish to speak to Mr. Lionel Stewart. The matter is urgent."

"I'll put you through Detective."

A male voice answered. "Detective Connors, this is Lionel Stewart. What is this urgent matter?"

"Yes Mr. Stewart. I am looking for your daughter Amanda."

"What the blazes has she done this time? That girl is nothing but trouble."

"Well sir, at this point I simply need to locate her. I require her to come to Nova Scotia for an interview. I hoped you might know where to reach her."

"She is in Cozumel. Got a call from her yesterday wanting more money. Let me look after this. When and where do you need her to be? Give me an idea what this is about. I expect I'll have to bring our lawyer."

"She was witness to a murder we had here last week. I need to see her this week, at my office in Tantallon."

"Is she a suspect? Did she kill someone this time? Never mind. We'll be there Wednesday afternoon. Nearest airport is?"

"No she is not a suspect. Stanfield International, Halifax is close."

"Will call you when we are landing." The line went dead.

Eli often dealt with odd characters. But this man topped the list. With that in mind, Eli would ensure that calls from Lionel Stewart went through Cpl. Walters and not directly to him. His next challenge was waiting in Interrogation.

"What did that Jimmy Moore tell you? I was getting ready to take off. Makin' me wait. Typical cops!" Leland towered over Eli. "I got a business to run."

"Just to remind you Mr. Boutilier, you showed up here over one hour early for our appointment and from what I understand, verbally assaulted Mr. Moore."

"Don't see why you called me in anyway. I told that other cop everything I knew that night."

Eli's usual calm demeanor was being stretched to the limit. He was not looking forward to this interview despite the fact he knew it could be most illuminating, if he handled it smartly.

"Let's not waste time. I am required to inform you that this interview will be video recorded."

"No it won't. I know how you guys work turning things around. I want a lawyer."

Leland was up out of seat with his hand on the door.

"Mr. Boutilier if you want your lawyer present, that is not a problem. Make another appointment at the desk."

Eli knew from experience not to antagonize this type of man. Little did Leland realize he was added to Eli's list of persons of interest.

Eli sat back down at his desk to note his impressions of the call with Lionel Stewart. He rewound the interview with Jimmy and began to make notes. Sal interrupted him.

"Buddy there said to tell you his lawyer would be in touch. Eli, he is a quite a piece of work!"

"Thanks Sal. The interview could not have gone better. I got what I needed for now." Eli grinned. "Sometimes less is more. I'm taking off in a few minutes. Bruce Matthews is coming in tomorrow." Eli was anxious to get home.

"I know he called to confirm this morning when you were with Jimmy. I put a note in your box. Asked if ten in the morning was still okay. I told him yes, unless you called him."

"Perfect. I am expecting a call on Wednesday from Lionel Stewart. When he calls, make an appointment for anytime that is good for him. Do not put him through to me. You will understand when you talk to him."

* * *

Bruce Matthews was early the next morning. Sal rang Eli to announce his arrival.

"I'll meet him in Interrogation." Eli closed the file he was working on and picked up the one on Bruce Matthews.

"Mr. Matthews, this interview will be videotaped."

"I understand that is standard procedure. If I may, I wish to make a statement before I answer your questions."

"As long as the content is relevant, I have no problem with that. Whenever you are ready." Eli pushed 'Record'.

"I grew up on Mackerel Point Road. I was known then as Jaime Mason. The man that was murdered was my uncle."

Eli reacted on a gut level. He realized that this was the person Beth fell in love with years ago. And, was the person who abandoned her.

Never, never, never mix business with your personal life.

"I knew Beth Johnston very well. I never loved another person like I still love Beth. I took a chance last week when I went to Pat Murphy's. The place was so busy that she did not recognize me. Or at least that is what I try to tell myself. I hadn't seen her in twenty-five years. She is as beautiful now as she was then. I was so young. I left her when she needed me."

Eli fought his emotions. He needed air. He put the video on 'Pause'.

"Mr. Matthews, I must excuse myself for a moment." Standing, hoping his legs would carry him, he headed for the rear entrance to the building.

Take deep breaths, Eli, deep breaths. You can and will do this. The truth is simply that. Get back in there. You are a cop. I warned you.

Eli straightened his shoulders.

"Sorry about that Mr. Matthews. Nature called. So, which name do you prefer, Bruce Matthews or Jaime Mason for the purpose of this interview?" Eli cloaked himself in his professional persona. He activated the recording.

"I have been Bruce Matthews for more than two decades Detective. I legally changed my name, as did my mother. Please call me Bruce."

"I understand you are here in Nova Scotia to settle your mother's estate. In the interview with Detective Rutherford on the night of the murder you stated that you did not recognize the victim on the night of the crime. Is that correct?"

"Yes, that is correct. That is what I told him. The man's appearance was not how I remembered my Uncle Leon."

"When was the last time you saw your uncle and what were the circumstances?"

"In April of 1986 I saw my uncle in the garage located at my home on Mackerel Point Road. I went out west that day and I never saw him again."

Beth had told Eli of the full circumstances of that day. Against his better judgment he did not ask Bruce to elaborate.

"Mr. Matthews, you drove your vehicle from British Columbia to Nova Scotia. You arrived in Halifax on what date?"

"I arrived in Halifax on March 15th of this year."

"And you chose to stay at the Harbour Inn instead of your family home on Mackerel Point Road. Why?"

"The place hasn't been lived in for several years. While in summer the house was always comfortable, at this time of year the rooms are very cold. I chose the comfort of the local Inn."

"You own a motorcycle repair business in British Columbia. Is that correct?"

"I do. And I am very proud of it. I teach at the college and offer students an entry point into the work force."

"So obviously you are more than familiar with the tools of your trade. Is an ice pick a useful tool for your line of work?"

"Oh yes. All mechanics use them. When I was a kid we used to find all kinds of uses for them. I have all my students add one to their kit, mainly for working on tires."

Bruce became much more animated when discussing his trade than on his initial presentation.

"One last question, do you recognize the name Amanda Stewart?"

"Not a name that I recall. Is she a local?"

"Thank you Mr. Matthews. You may go. However, you may be contacted again. I request that you not leave the province until I or a court representative authorize you to do so."

*   *   *

The Coroner's office was asking whether Leon Mason's body would be claimed or should their office arrange for disposal of the remains. In his search for family Eli was disappointed to learn Trent Mason had died three months ago in northern New Brunswick. Shortly after the murder Eli spoke with Leon and Trent's sister, Susan. She refused to have anything to do with her dead brother when Eli contacted her.

"No good son of a bitch will burn in hell for what he done." Were her words to him. He notified the Coroner to dispose of the body in due course.

Eli gathered the case files including the transcript of Leon's 1999 trial. A theory was forming in his mind.

"I'm taking work home Sal. Remember Lionel Stewart will be calling. My cell is on."

"Don't stay up all night in that think tank of yours."

Eli enjoyed his tiny cottage. He built it himself the summer he got his posting to the area. The small lot was situated on Paul's Point Road by the water. His sixty feet of shoreline consisted of hundreds of various sized granite stones all rolled smooth from the continuous breaking of waves. His cottage was a simple two-story box with a combined kitchen and living space with a woodstove for heat and cooking. A Spartan bathroom was also on the ground floor. Tall windows embraced the entire wall facing the open ocean. A ladder connected the two floors. Upstairs was one room, a king-sized bed to the right and a desk area to the left.

His favorite part of the house was what Sal referred to as his think tank. His desk looked out over the Bay. A weathered leather overstuffed chair he'd had since his college days sat beside his desk. Eli would settle into that chair, put his feet up on the windowsills and listen to the rocks moving on the shore with every wave. Here he did his thinking.

Eli had told two very important people he would be in touch with them on Tuesday evening. He intended to keep his word. He called Ali first.

"Hello."

"Ali?"

"Yes. Is that you Detective Connors"

"It is. My cell reception can be poor out here."

"Thank you for calling, I have been waiting. Was the information I gave you helpful? And before I forget to say, Halifax is as charming a city as you said."

"I thought you would find it so. And to answer your question, the information you brought to me was very helpful. I can tell you that I expect to meet Amanda Stewart sometime tomorrow. How are you doing?"

"Oh, I'm fine but better now that you called. Will I be able to talk to Amanda?"

"I'm not certain that would be wise just yet Ali, for either of you. Let me interview her, try to get a feel for the situation. I have all of the information you gave me."

"Detective Connors just tell me, is Beth Johnston my mother? I know that is unfair to ask you. But I am so tempted to just rent a car and drive out to Indian Harbour. I've read the newspaper articles. I make my living asking questions. The only thing holding me back is that I don't want to screw up your investigation."

"Thankfully! Just give me another day. Let me talk to Amanda. Ali, let me do my job. I will call you as soon as I think I am able to give you more definitive answers. This case has become very complicated."

"I hear what you are saying." Alison did not give up easily. "But . . . I think my father was the man who was murdered and my mother is Beth Johnston who owns the place where he was killed. And if Amanda wrote to her like she did to me, she must be as confused as I am. If she had to give us away when we were born and worse if she wonders whether or not her two babies stayed together . . . seriously Detective, do you blame me for wanting to know?"

"You are a smart woman. Please leave this with me for another day. I promise I have your best interests in mind. I will call you again tomorrow night." Eli tried to maintain as professional voice as he could. Then lamely added, "If you're into museums, the Museum of Natural History has a famous dinosaur on display this month. And the Art Gallery down the street from you is worthwhile."

"Nice try. I'll wait for your call. Bye for now." She hung up.

He called Beth's cell phone.

I'm busy. Leave a message.

Never was he so glad to leave a message.

Beth, it's Eli. Told you I would call tonight. Will try to reach you tomorrow, at the latest Thursday evening.

Then he climbed the ladder to his think tank and was awake until sunrise. But the time was well spent.

Eli's next move was to consult the Crown Prosecutor. At the very least he could present the case as he saw it and request the warrants he required. Meeting with the Crown Prosecutor always reminded Eli of being called to the Principal's office as a youth. His palms and armpits were soaked as he sat outside the office.

He need not have been so anxious. In fact, he was commended for the speed with which he brought forward his theory. The warrants he requested were obtained from a judge even before he left the office.

His cell phone rang as walked to his car. "Detective Connors."

"Cpl. Walters here. I see what you meant about that Stewart guy. I set up an appointment this afternoon but he expected to see you now."

"Sal, you're always on it. I'll be at the office within the hour. I have the search warrants in my hands."

"I'll start the process from this end so you can execute them ASAP. Bye."

* * *

"Mr. Stewart, I'm Detective Connors."

Nodding his head toward his companions, "My daughter Amanda and our lawyer, Maxwell Weatherby. Let's get started shall we."

Fellow definitely has presence, Eli thought. "Certainly. We'll be in the conference room down the hall. Detective Rutherford, my partner will be joining us."

Lionel Stewart, despite his small stature filled a room. Amanda spoke not a word. Seating themselves around the conference table, Eli took the lead. Earlier he arranged the chairs, his briefcase on the table at the head of the table.

"My daughter has been mentally unwell for many years and continues to be under the care of a team of psychiatric specialists. Over the course of the past twenty-four hours she disclosed to Mr. Weatherby and I the activities which have amused her since being released from hospital. She admits to some mischief concerning Alison McLaughlin. Amanda has been medicated and not capable of answering questions at this point. I plan to return to Vancouver today with her. I will see that she receives appropriate psychiatric care. In the meantime I am sure we can work out an arrangement regarding a future interview." Lionel Stewart's voice remained authoritative.

"I am arresting Amanda Stewart for Identity Fraud, today." Eli paused. He saw a small smile budding on Amanda's face.

"And, as she is now a person of interest in the murder of Leon Mason she will not be leaving this province today." Eli finished.

Amanda laughed out loud. "Touché Detective Connors! Will I be spending the night in a jail cell? How exciting Daddy, don't you think?"

Eli ignored Lionel Stewart's protests. Calmly walking to his office he closed the door.

* * *

Jenna answered the home telephone.

"Hello, Jenna. This is Detective Connors calling. I am out your way. We were not able to finish our interview on the weekend. I wish to do so now."

"Adam isn't here so I don't think now is a good time."

"Actually I wanted to talk to you. I can speak with Adam at a later date. We're just pulling into your driveway."

Jenna felt more annoyed than worried. Earlier, Adam decided to take a drive down the shore to check on the project site, dropping Sylvie at playschool on his way.

She opened the door for Eli and his partner.

"I apologize for the short notice Jenna."

"No matter, you're here. You have questions for me?"

"Yes, about your inventory in the shop. Do you have a list available?"

"I do. The computer with the information is out in the shop. I'll get my coat. I closed today for a well-deserved day off. Are you looking for something in particular?"

"Let's just have a look." They followed her along the path and into the attractive building.

"Chilly in here. Will this take long?" Jenna began to get anxious as she looked at him. Turning on the computer, she sat down at the desk.

"Depends on the size of the list."

The screen displayed the shop logo. Within seconds Jenna brought up her inventory file.

"There is the folder Detectives. You can find what I have now, what has been sold and what I plan to purchase. But if you simply tell me what you are looking for, I can tell you whether or not I have it."

"Like I said, let me just have a look first." Eli quite intended to ask the question but wanted to watch Jenna's reaction to his enquiry before he did. He clicked on the file titled Current. The items appeared in the order of the dates of procurement with detailed information about each, including a number likely matching the tags he noticed were tied to the articles on display.

"Quite an organized system you have here! You pay great attention to detail. So Jenna, do you have or have you ever listed an ice pick?"

"You think I killed that awful man!"

"Please answer my question."

"I may have. My assistant does the cataloguing and some of the buying. Let me look." She took over the mouse, opened another document titled categories and entered a search. Three results appeared.

"The answer is yes as you can see. Two have been sold and one should be in the storage room in the basement of our house." The colour drained from Jenna's face. "Do I need a lawyer?"

"You certainly have the right to call one Jenna. But I do have warrant to seize your computer and search the premises."

*   *   *

Thursday dawned overcast, hinting that the sunshine of the previous few days were soon to be replaced with Nova Scotia's winter weather.

A storm was brewing. Eli could feel it in more ways than one. Today he was to meet with Leland Boutilier and his lawyer.

Ali's message left on his cell phone late last night, spoke of her impatience.

The RCMP computer tech left a pile of printouts on his desk from Jenna's computer.

The ice pick found in the Reynoldz storage room turned out to be a tool used by cliff climbers and was sitting on his credenza. Adam refused further interview without a lawyer present.

This could be quite a day!

Sal knocked on his door.

"Come in."

"Like seeing a ghost Eli, it's like seeing a ghost! Alison McLaughlin is in the waiting room. Until she spoke I figured Amanda escaped the shrinks." Sal shook her head. "She insists she see you, now."

"Show her in. God knows what she'll do if I don't. When is Boutilier coming?"

"At eleven, in an hour. Interrogation room is ready. The Crown's office said a prosecutor would be here by ten-thirty. I heard from the Forensic Unit at the hospital. They'll call when Amanda's preliminary evaluation is done. They thought by four. Anything else?"

"Yes, I think I better talk to Alison in the conference room. Anyone in there?"

"No, it's free. I'll bring her down there."

Eli knew he couldn't stall Ali much longer. Though DNA matching remained as the gold standard to prove the relationship between Alison, Amanda, Beth and Leon Mason, Eli knew what the results would show. His dilemma was when to have the tests done. As his theory began to take shape he hoped to avoid that legal requirement.

In the conference room Ali was pacing. Closing the door behind him, Eli pulled out a chair.

Ali turned. "I had to come. Thank you for seeing me. I know you must be busy."

"Never mind. Believe me, I understand. Have seat. I'm going to tell you something, not everything, but enough for your purpose. Before I do, I need your word that you will not act on the knowledge today."

"I give you my word Detective Connors."

He told her relevant bits and pieces of the information Beth had given him on Saturday night. He did not mention Jaime, Leon or the night of the murder.

"When can I meet Beth?

"Soon."

ARREST

April 16, 2011

A presentably attired Leland Boutilier and his lawyer, Alan Jones sat on the far side of the table in the interrogation room. Eli informed them that the interview was being recorded.

"Mr. Boutilier, you were interviewed here on the night of March 16th of this year following the murder of Leon Mason. Is that correct?" Eli held the typed copy of the interview.

"Yeah, but I was pretty loaded."

"Was Leon Mason your brother-in-law?"

"Yeah."

"So you lied to the detective who interviewed you on March 16th. You said you did not recognize the victim."

"I guess so. Like I said I was pretty loaded."

"Did you recognize him when he stopped your truck on the wharf road earlier that same afternoon?"

"Yeah."

"Was your brother-in-law found guilty of assaulting and raping your daughter twelve years ago? And did he go to prison as a result?"

Leland looked at the lawyer who indicated his client should answer the question.

"Yeah."

This lawyer has done a good job preparing his client, Eli thought and was impressed.

"Do the tools used on a lobster boat include an ice pick?"

Leland leaned over and again asked his lawyer a question.

Looking uncomfortable, Leland nodded. "Yeah."

"Tell me Mr. Boutilier, why did you insist on joining Jimmy Moore when Beth Johnston asked only for Jimmy's help after the pub closed?"

Alan Jones spoke. "Don't answer that."

He rose to his feet. "My client has co-operated. He made it clear to you that he was under the influence of alcohol on the evening of March 16th. He has corrected the errors he made during the previous interview. If you intend to charge my client with a crime, do it now. Otherwise this interview is over."

"Very well Mr. Jones." Eli's cell phone rang. "Excuse while I answer this. Give me a couple of minutes. Please wait."

Eli joined the Crown Prosecutor in the recording room.

"Well, did they find one?"

"The search of *Evie*, Leland Boutilier's lobster boat did not reveal an ice pick. However, while Leland said such an item is used, you did not ask if he used one on his boat. The good news is that when asked, a member of his crew told the officer, '*Must be around here somewhere.'* Go ahead. Arrest Boutilier. I'll take it from there." Erin McIsaac was taking on his first murder case as a Crown Attorney.

Eli and Cpl. Walters entered Interrogation. Eli read Leland Boutilier his rights, while Cpl. Walters placed the handcuffs. She led him off to a holding cell.

"What! I didn't kill him. Alan tell him they can't arrest an innocent man. Do something you asshole. I did what you said. I said what you told me to say!" Leland raged.

"If you know what's good for you, keep your mouth shut Leland. I'll see you downtown." Alan Jones picked up his briefcase. "I'll wait for the paperwork Detective Connors."

Eli would work closely with the Crown on this case. He was aware that the case against Leland was largely circumstantial. He had contacted another potential witness whom he would question in the days to come. But he did not have any hard evidence for the Crown.

RELATIONSHIPS

E li called Beth's cell phone.

"This is Beth." Her perky voice responded.

"Hi Beth, Eli here. I need to see you. How busy are you?"

"Not very. Are you coming out?"

"I would like to, but will we be able to speak privately?"

"Marg is here. She can watch the bar for a bit and close early, no one is here anyway. Come to the house. Do you know where I live?"

"Yes. I'll be there in twenty minutes."

Beth's cottage sat on a rise behind Pat Murphy's Pub. The one and a half story structure was clad in white clapboard. Wooden shutters of a deep blue adorned the windows, in contrast to the bright red front door and its hand painted welcome sign. A swirl of grey smoke rose from the chimney.

Beth opened the door as Eli drove into the driveway. Her natural beauty took his breath away as she waved beckoning him into her home.

"Right on time! I made a pot of coffee and Marg insisted that I bring over a pot of chowder and fresh rolls." Beth smiled.

The mix of aromas was intoxicating for Eli. Maintaining a somewhat professional demeanor took all of his emotional strength.

"Thanks for seeing me on such short notice Beth. Great spot you have here."

"Hmm, you have on your detective voice. Come on out to the kitchen."

The place was a reflection of Beth. Warm earth tones, local art on the walls, a small kitchen with an antique wood cook stove and a variety of plants hanging in the windows, some of which Eli recognized as herbs.

Despite himself, Eli could not help but comment. "Your home is so you Beth, beautiful in every sense of the word."

"Why, thank you. But I realize that you are bringing me some news. Shall we start with that?"

"Of course." Eli sat at the table; Beth chose the rocking chair beside the stove.

"Well?" Beth was curious. "I'm getting nervous vibes. Should I be worried Eli?"

"No. I hope I am bringing news that will answer many questions. First, I can tell you that Leland Boutilier has been arrested for the murder of Leon Mason."

"What! Leland?"

"Yes, but I cannot say more than that at this point. But that is not my main purpose in seeing you now."

"Oh Eli, what is it?"

"Beth, when you told me last week about your teen years I had some information that I could not share with you then. Let me come straight to the point. I have met your twin daughters. In fact you met one of them on the night of March 16th." He did not mention Jaime or Adam. Eli paused, watching Beth's reaction.

"The girl at the pub that night who looked vaguely familiar is one of my daughters!" Beth stopped rocking, stood up and wandered into in the living room. Eli followed.

"You met both of my girls? Where are they? Are they okay? My God Eli." Beth's tears began.

After he told her what he knew about Amanda and Alison, Eli held Beth in his arms.

"Eli, I want to see Alison."

"She is waiting for my call."

Beth pulled away from his embrace. "Call her, now. Will she talk to me?"

Eli dialed Ali's number. She picked up on the first ring.

"Detective Connors?"

"Yes Ali, its me."

"Did you tell her? Are you with her now? Will she see me?"

"Yes. Beth wants to speak to you. Shall I hand over the phone?"

Beth grabbed the phone. "Ali, this is Beth. Are you okay?"

Eli would never forget watching the birth of a relationship that took place before his eyes. He saw Beth's range of emotion; heard her kind understanding words and saw amazement as she realized that her daughter wanted to be a part of her life.

With tears of joy Beth turned to face Eli. "She is coming here, now. One of my babies is coming home."

Beth paced in silence by the front door. Car lights turning into the driveway illuminated the hall. Beth opened the door as her daughter stepped onto the porch. Ali had arrived.

"Welcome Alison, I'm Beth."

Eli stood mesmerized as the two women immediately and comfortably embraced. He excused himself quickly with a smile and his characteristic nod to each of them. Beth and Alison's reunion was easy. He knew if and when Amanda joined them the situation was unlikely to be as cordial.

As he drove home that night he was well aware that he had fallen hopelessly in love with Beth Johnston. He desperately wanted her in his life.

*　　*　　*

The next morning Eli entered his office just as his desk phone began to ring. Dropping his briefcase beside his chair he reached for the receiver. "Detective Connors speaking." He shrugged off his jacket and hung it on the back of his chair.

"This is Dr. Wells at the Abbey Lane Hospital in Halifax. I apologize for not calling yesterday about Amanda Stewart."

"No problem Dr. Wells. The case is complicated, I understand. What can you tell me?"

"As you know, a patient can be held up to thirty days for a complete assessment. Yesterday I encountered a problem when the patient's father arrived in my office with the psychiatrist in charge of Amanda's care in Vancouver. Mr. Stewart also brought his lawyer. As a result I found it necessary to call upon the hospital's legal counsel. We are now engaged in legal wrangling about where and with who

Ms. Stewart will be further assessed. For now she continues to be an inpatient under my care. However, I have been advised not to allow the RCMP to question her at this time, though that had been my intention following my interview with her."

Eli caught the innuendo. "So we wait. I am not surprised. I appreciate your call, and your position. Can someone keep me up to date with the progress? I would prefer to have Ms Stewart available for questioning in Nova Scotia."

"I will do my best. I have made our lawyer aware of your needs. Sorry that I can't tell you more."

"What you have told me is helpful. Thanks." So the barrier was not Amanda's mental state but her father's wish to whisk her back to BC and avoid unpleasant press. Eli would need to consult with the Crown. There was no doubt that Amanda had committed identity fraud. Both professionally and personally he wanted the process to proceed without delay.

*   *   *

That afternoon Eli was meeting with the Crown Attorney, Erin McIsaac in Halifax to present his written report on the case, prior to Leland Boutilier's arraignment. He expected Leland to enter a plea of not guilty.

He planned to push for Leland to be held on remand until trial, given the nature of the charge and Leland's criminal record of assault. Eli was concerned for witness safety, in particular, Jimmy Moore. Erin agreed with Eli's concerns regarding remand.

Reviewing the summary of Eli's report, Erin had questions about the circumstantial nature of the case. In particular, the murder weapon worried him; and the toxicology results from the coroner's investigation indicating the presence of benzodiazepines was not explained to his satisfaction. Eli would be required to continue his investigation on those points.

At arraignment Leland did plead not guilty. The judge agreed with the Crown and ordered that Leland be remanded until trial. No bail hearing would be heard.

The trial was scheduled to begin on the 20th of September.

*   *   *

Eli went home, called for a delivery pizza and donned comfortable clothes. His thoughts were of Beth. He flipped on his sound system, turning the volume to the point of shaking the windows. Settling into his favorite chair with the intention to tune out he suddenly realized would not hear any knock on his door, or the ring of his cell phone he'd left on the kitchen table. He bolted from the chair. Sliding down the ladder, landing on the floor barefoot he grabbed his phone. Sure enough, he had missed a call. Beth had left a message.

Eli, call me when you get this message.

Great! Eli felt like a fifteen-year-old boy; he dialed her number.

"Hi Eli. That was fast. Are you on the road?"

"No, I'm home. Had the music up too loud." An unfamiliar anxiety gripped him. "What's up? How did it go with Ali last night after I left?"

"You mean after you escaped!" Beth chuckled. "I need to talk to you about last night. Can I come over? Alison has gone to get her things. She will start staying at my place tomorrow."

"Sure you can come over." Eli panicked inside.

"I'm on my way." Beth hung up.

*   *   *

Beth knocked on the back door as she opened it. Stepping into his kitchen she was amazed.

"Wow Eli, great place!"

"I like it." He laughed. "Welcome to my world."

"What a fantastic view." Beth moved to the living room windows and stood with her hands on her hips.

An awkward silence filled the room.

Eli spoke first. "You said you wanted to talk about last night."

She turned. "I do. I have a question."

Eli extended his hand, "Have seat. Would you like something to drink?"

"Do you have any red wine?" Beth chose to sit on the wide windowsill.

"Merlot okay?"

"Perfect."

Eli poured two glasses, passed one to Beth and settled himself on the sill beside her.

"Cheers." Eli was having difficulty reading Beth's mood.

"Eli we need to have a serious discussion about what is happening between us." While her words were confident, her voice betrayed her vulnerability. "At least I have to be honest with you about my feelings."

Eli's mind reeled. At a loss for words he could only nod.

"This is embarrassing. I have romantic feelings for you. And I may be wrong but I think you have the same for me. I can feel it."

"You aren't wrong Beth. I am falling in love with you. In our situation this is way beyond inappropriate. We do need to talk about that."

"And something else." Beth desperately wanted to have him embrace her again, but was determined to hold back until her concerns were addressed. "When you were telling me about Ali and Amanda, I sensed you had more to say."

"I did. I should say, I do. I'm not sure when the right time is. But I knew it was not then." Eli reached for her hand, turning to look into her eyes. "Amanda was not the only person from your past who was in Pat Murphy's that night. Beth, Jaime was there."

"No! I would have known him. Eli that can't be." Beth grabbed her hand away from him, stood and began to pace. "Anything else?"

"Gina's son Adam was there, with his wife."

"I'm going to be sick." She ran to the kitchen and leaned over the sink.

Eli opened the door to the deck and stepped outside. The moon cast a golden shadow across the Bay; the broken, receding waves dragged the beach stones into the sea with the familiar tumbling sound. The spring wind was cool. He heard his father's words again, *Never, never, never mix business with your personal life!* On this night the old man added, *or be prepared to pay the price.*

Quietly, Eli finally answered the ghost. "I am prepared. I am not you."

*　*　*

In lockup Leland Boutilier was furious. He directed his rage toward Detective Eli Connors. He was unable to reconcile being locked up for six months.

Despite Alan Jones reassurance that the case against him was circumstantial, that at trial he was confident of acquittal, Leland continued to be aggressive.

The guards recorded threats toward Detective Connors.

"I'll make that son of a bitch pay when I get out of here."

* * *

Amanda Stewart's arraignment for Identity Theft proved to be a fiasco. The judge read the charge. Maxwell Weatherby and Amanda stood. The lawyer entered a plea of 'not guilty'. His client had other ideas.

Appealing to the judge, in a loud voice Amanda cried, "No, Wait! I am guilty. I did impersonate my twin sister Alison McLaughlin. I should be punished. My father with all of his wealth always bails me out of trouble. The time has come for me to take responsibility for my actions."

Silence fell over the courtroom.

Lionel Stewart's face contorted with rage. "You ungrateful bitch! You'll pay for this embarrassment." With Maxwell Weatherby in tow, Lionel stormed out of the courtroom.

Amanda felt an invigorating surge of adrenalin. "Please excuse my father. He behaves badly when he loses control of me."

The judge's gavel sounded. " The accused pleads guilty to the charge. Sentencing will take place one week from today. Next case."

Amanda was pleased with herself. She knew she could go to prison for six months. How bad could that be? Giving up her passport to the court didn't worry her.

In the back of the courtroom, Eli nudged his partner and smiled. "Go get her." Detectives Connors and Rutherford were to conduct the long overdue interview with Amanda Stewart, a suspect for the March 16th murder of Leon Mason.

Amanda verified designing a plan to bring her cousin, her twin sister, their mother and Leon Mason together. She denied any malicious intent. Claiming a lifelong, obsessive desire to find her family of origin, she confessed that her approach was in poor taste.Leaving the Courthouse, Amanda flipped open her cell phone. When her PI answered she simply said, "Set it up."

The desk clerk at the Prince George became confused when Amanda registered. "Ms. McLaughlin, you're back. We thought you were in Indian Harbour. Would you like the same room?"

Amanda was tempted to continue the charade but replied, "I am Alison's twin sister, Amanda Stewart. Everyone gets us confused. The same room my sister had is fine. Thank you. Oh, and I'll be dining out after I unpack."

*   *   *

Driving back to St. Margaret's Bay Eli thought about Beth and the information he gave her and what he did not. She didn't know what had happened to Gina Mason and Jaime's mother. Nor was she aware that her daughter, Amanda was going to prison. He and Beth had not spoken in over a week. Today was Friday. He had the weekend to himself. Eli decided the time had come to see her again. Dropping by Pat Murphy's was a place to start.

Pushing open the pub's heavy oak door Eli slipped inside. Several tables were full and three young men sat at the bar laughing with the bartender. A smiling Alison was charming those patrons when she looked over to see who entered. Eli was relieved that she waved. He saw Marg come down the stairs to deliver meals. He caught her eye. And she smiled. Eli made his way to the bar.

"What will you have?" Ali asked.

"Keith's draught please."

"Yes sir! About time you came by to see my new talent! I'll run you a tab." Ali filled the glass like a pro. "The boss is upstairs in the office. Go on up."

As he passed Marg she told him, "Top of the stairs on the right. Good luck."

Eli knocked on the closed door.

"Come on in."

He hesitated. "Beth, its Eli."

Silence.

She opened the door wide and stood staring at him.

"You have now seen how I behave when I am overwhelmed." She stepped forward to face him eye to eye. "I am so glad to see you."

"I'm glad to see you too. I am sorry. You are an amazing woman, even when you are overwhelmed." Eli was anxious and determined tell her all of what he knew of her family.

"Not so fast Eli." Beth ushered him into the office. "We need privacy."

"I have more to tell you Beth; more about Jaime, his family and about Amanda."

"Wait! Before you start. I went to see Jaime at the Harbour Inn. I know all about Lil, Gina and Adam. Most importantly, I know that whatever adolescent romantic feelings I once had for Jaime have gone. I consider him a coward and I told him so. Our meeting was not pleasant. But I faced him. He had no reasonable explanation for abandoning his family and me.

Beth took a deep breath and continued. "He finished the business that brought him back to Nova Scotia. That awful property is for sale. He left some time today for the West Coast."

"Ali has told me about Amanda's background and her deceptions. So right now all I care about knowing is news about that wayward daughter. And, to tell you that I do love you."

Eli's anxiety dissolved, "I love you too Beth. We will get through this mess, I promise."

Their embrace was natural and comforting for them both; their kiss promised a future to be explored.

"That was very nice Detective Connors! But . . . what is happening with Amanda?"

"Amanda has been charged with Identity Fraud, pled guilty in court and will be sentenced next week."

"Is she in jail?"

"No, not now but she will be. The court took her passport. I assume she is still somewhere in Halifax. My guess is that her father and his lawyer flew back to BC washing their hands of her. It was quite a show in court."

"Ali and I want to meet with her."

"You mean before sentencing?"

"Yes."

"I'm not sure that is such a good idea Beth. You can't imagine how completely different she is from Alison."

"Let's go talk to Ali. She has some interesting thoughts about her sister." Beth embraced him and planted a kiss on his cheek.

Ali was washing glasses when Eli and Beth came down. The supper crowd gone, the pub was empty.

"So did you two patch things up?" Ali quipped.

"Where's your three admirers gotten to?" Eli came back.

"Smarty! I sent them packing. Now answer my question."

"We kissed and made up, yes." Beth took a seat on a barstool.

"Why are you down here then?" Ali winked at Eli.

Beth was serious. "Amanda pled guilty about impersonating you. She isn't in jail yet. Eli says she will be sentenced next week. I want you to tell Eli your reasons for wanting to see her."

Ali put down the dishtowel. "Since I was a little girl I've had nightmares. The dream is always the same. I think the theme has to do with Amanda. Meeting her might take it away. Plus I am curious. She obviously knows some of the missing pieces to our history; things Beth doesn't know."

Eli neither saw nor heard any malice in Ali.

Beth added, "While this may sound creepy, I have a similar nightmare. I don't have the expectation that it will go away in the same way Ali does. But if Amanda can or will tell us what she knows about their adoption, I want to know."

"I understand that." Eli paused. "But what I know of Amanda is that she is very manipulative. You'll need to be careful."

"Like you're telling me something I don't know!" Ali picked up the bar phone and dialed. "I just wonder."

"Hello. This is Alison McLaughlin speaking. I stayed with you at the Prince George when I first arrived in Halifax."

She fidgeted as she listened to the desk clerk's response.

"Yes, everyone says that about us. We haven't seen each other in a long time. Do me a favor; don't tell her I called. I want to surprise her. Do you know if she is in?"

Beth and Eli were incredulous. Looking at each other, both said, "How did she know?"

"Thanks. I really appreciate it." Ali's hand shook as she put down the phone.

Looking at Eli she laughed, "I just had a hunch she'd pick that hotel. Call it some sort of paranormal communication! She even took the same room. But she did give her own name."

"You didn't have your call put through."

"No. She isn't in. Unfortunately she knows I am visiting out here in the Bay. I would have preferred to have the upper hand when we first met." Ali's mood was not so light hearted. "I expect she will find us."

Ali's words were barely spoken when the outside bell rang, the pub's door opened and Amanda breezed in nonchalantly.

"Isn't this just a quaint scene." Amanda strolled up to the bar. "Detective Connors, off duty I assume. Beth, I am Amanda. And Alison, I'd obviously recognize you anywhere!"

A palpable hush fell. Beth was relieved the pub was empty. She took the time to compose herself, flipping the window sign to 'Closed' and locking the door.

"Amanda, we've been expecting you." Eli broke the silence.

"Of course! That cute little cop you have tailing me." Amanda seated herself on a barstool facing her sister. "I'll have a glass of water barkeeper. You are more attractive than your picture by the way."

Turning to Beth, "Shall I call you Mother, or Mommy?" Amanda quipped.

Nonplussed and fully aware of Amanda's 'hurt or be hurt' defense, Beth leaned on the bar to directly face her daughter. "I will remain 'Beth' to you. And, I will not tolerate your diva act here."

Rarely was Amanda called on her behavior. She quickly considered her options. "I understand you. I promise to behave appropriately." Holding Beth's gaze, she challenged, "Not that my promises have ever been worth much."

Touche. Beth thought. *She has a quick mind but little personal insight.* "Thank you. We all appreciate that."

Ali was not prepared to be so conciliatory. "Personally, I find your behaviour very offensive Amanda."

Amanda stood back, her hands on her hips. "Well, well, listen to our 'little Miss Perfect. Is that all you have to say?"

A deep sadness descended over Beth. Watching her daughters she thought, *Dear Ali, you are no match for her in this game. Be smarter.*

Eli was keenly aware of the dynamic developing in the room. With a theatrical sweeping gesture he burst out, " Ladies, ladies, drop your weapons or I'll have to call the cops!"

Despite themselves the look on his face caused the women to dissolve in fits of laughter.

*   *   *

Adam and Jenna were having problems. While their daughter, Sylvie continued to struggle with her developmental delays, her mother expressed increasing frustration to her husband. In fact she began to blame Adam for the child's difficulties.

"Why didn't you investigate your background?" Jenna said after putting Sylvie to bed one evening. "She is never going to keep up with other kids. I never would have had a child if I'd known."

"What do you expect me to say Jenna? Lots of children have problems." Adam was shocked by the changes he was seeing in his wife since their meeting with Amanda Stewart.

"And you've dragged me into a murder investigation! What kind of family do you come from? I want nothing to do with them. Your 'parents' are lovely, normal people. Did they know about you? Why didn't they tell me?" Jenna's voice shook.

"Jenna, please. I am the same guy you met and married." Adam searched for words. "We have a wonderful home, a beautiful daughter and an enviable life. Challenges come up. I can't change that. I'm upset too."

"What good is that? You go off to work; spend days out on the site. I'm stuck here trying to run a business and cope with Sylvie." Jenna was angry. "I got a subpoena to court today. You and that bitch Amanda have ruined my life!"

"Subpoena? Was Amanda charged?"

"Get your head out of your ass Adam! No you fool. Leland Boutilier was charged with murder. Don't you ever listen to the news? I've been called as a witness for the Crown."

* * *

Bruce was aware that he should have contacted Detective Connors before leaving the province. Instead he left a message with the officer on duty. He was clear in the message that he would return if required.

He needed to get home. The hurtful memories multiplied after he met with Beth. She was so cold and heartless despite his sincere apologies for leaving her. He did not recognize her. She refused to listen to him about his reasons, his pain.

She was only concerned with what became of his mother and sister. She refused to share any information about her own life and ignored his attempts to discuss his accomplishments.

He knew she would never forgive him no matter what restitution he made. His heart was broken.

*   *   *

Amanda was amazed to see Beth and Alison in the corridor outside courtroom on the day of her sentencing. Her public defender asked Amanda if Alison might speak on her behalf. Amanda told her that was unlikely to happen.

Both Ali and Beth approached Amanda, and her lawyer.

Beth began, "Amanda, Ali and I appreciate the honesty with which you spoke to us on the weekend, even though we had a rough start. You stayed. You shared the knowledge we lacked. Your sister and I understand you a lot better now."

"So if either of us can help you today, we have agreed to do so." Ali finished. "I am moving my work to Nova Scotia so I will be here to support you, if you need or want that."

Amanda was stunned. She felt guilt for the first time in her life; the feeling was not comfortable. She prided herself on her inability to feel anything. Her plan was founded on that ability.

Her lawyer was quick to step in. He asked if Ali would make a statement to the court.

"I will do that." Ali looked to her left at her sister. Amanda looked away.

*   *   *

Ali's statement and appearance in court influenced the judge's decision. He reduced Amanda's sentence from the maximum six months to four months in the local minimum-security facility. She would be released early in September to be available for Leland Boutilier's trial should she be called to testify.

Amanda settled into her cell alone. The place was reminiscent of a rehab; except no shrink was trying to get into her head. The routine was simple; giving her plenty of time for planning. Ali and Beth came by to visit occasionally.

Alan Jones arrived in July to personally deliver a summons for her to appear as a defense witness in Leland Boutilier's trial. She was pleased and prepared to give him more than he needed.

By mid August Amanda was bored. No one of any interest to her had crossed her path. Then ten days before her release, an exotic dark haired beauty appeared as her cellmate.

One look at her and Amanda recognized the girl to be just what she needed.

"I'm Amanda. What's your name?"

"I am Ernesta." She eyed Amanda suspiciously.

Spanish, maybe Mexican. Amanda thought and turned on her charm. "Commo estas?"

"You speak Spanish?" The girl's rich accent was intriguing.

"Not very well I'm afraid! But I try." She knew immediately that this girl had a story to tell. "I have been here for a few months and it is not so bad."

"I arrived last night from Mexico to study at the university." Ernesta began to cry. "I don't understand. I am told I may be deported so they put me here."

"Oh no! But you won't be here very long. There are rules about that sort of thing."

"I attend el encuentro, a meeting in two days."

She wants to talk. Amanda offered, "Cómo puedo ayudarle?

TRIAL

September 20, 2011

With the jury selected, Erin McIsaac the Crown Attorney made his very brief opening remarks.

"Ladies and gentlemen of the jury, the Crown will prove that the accused, Leland Boutilier sitting here before you had the motive, the means and the opportunity to commit the murder of Leon Mason. And that he did so on the evening of March 16, 2011."

He called his first witness, Danny Boutilier to the stand. Erin McIsaac had interviewed all three of Leland's boys as potential witnesses. Danny was the more well spoken of the three, clearly recalled the events of March 16th and, he liked to hear himself talk. The two younger sons, Scott and Paul were uncooperative and belligerent.

"Mr. Boutilier, may I call you Danny?" Erin began.

"Sure, that's my name."

"Please tell the court the events that took place on the evening of March 16th of this year."

"My uncle got killed." Danny appeared pleased with himself.

"Let me be more specific. Did you see your uncle on the dock before he was murdered in Pat Murphy's Pub?"

"Yeah, but I didn't know who he was. When I was rowing in with my brothers I saw my dad almost run over an old white haired guy. Then the dude comes down on the dock as we were leaving trying to sell weed."

"You and your brothers then met your father at the pub. Is that correct?"

"Yes sir. The boat was secure. It was blowing hard that night. We were havin' a few brew, watchin' the weather channel on Beth's big screen. Then Jimmy came to get us after last call."

"Do you recall if your father, Leland Boutilier left the pub anytime between the time you met him there and the time you left with Jimmy Moore?"

"Well, we all were drinkin' pretty heavy. All of us went to the can a few times. He might've left the table to take a piss outside."

"Did your father put on his rain slicker and say that he was going to check the boat again before you all went home." In the interview with Danny the young man had offered this information.

"He might have."

"Please answer 'yes' or 'no'."

"Yes."

"And on stormy nights does Jimmy Moore drive by the dock before driving you home?"

"Yeah."

"On March 16th, did Jimmy drive by the dock?"

"No."

"Why was that Danny?"

"I don't know."

"Did your father, Leland Boutilier say not to bother; that he'd already checked the boat?

"He might have. I was sitting' in the back. Jimmy had the radio turned up loud."

Erin picked up the bagged murder weapon, asked the court to enter the ice pick as evidence and then showed it to the witness.

"Danny, do you know what this is?"

"Sure. We fix traps with them things."

"Were you present on your father's boat when investigators searched it?"

"Yeah."

"That day did they find this type tool?"

"I don't know what they did or didn't find. Don't know exactly what they were looking for."

"Danny do you understand the term 'perjury'?"

"Yeah. Okay, they were lookin' for an ice pick."

"Thank you." Walking toward the witness stand Erin said, "In the report submitted to the court, the one I now have in my hand, the lead investigator has written that she asked you personally whether or not such a tool was used on the boat, and that you answered *Sure. Must be one around here somewhere.* Is that correct?"

Danny was cocky until his eyes met his father's glaring back at him. Danny's voice lowered.

"Yeah, I said that." Then in a vain attempt to help his father, "But those things go missing all the time."

"Thank you Danny. That is all I have for this witness at this time. However, I reserve the ability to recall. Your witness Mr. Jones."

Alan Jones remained seated and put his hand on Leland's arm. "Kind of tough, isn't it Danny; being called to testify for a lawyer who wants to put your father in jail for murder?"

"Yeah."

"You have been working on the boat with your father for what, ten or fifteen years?"

"Full-time since I was seventeen. I'm twenty-seven my next birthday."

"And Danny how often would you say that a bad Nor'easter blows into the Bay?"

"Well, in the late summer hurricane season, that depends. But our boat isn't out much then anyway. In winter when we're putting out traps, maybe three, four times we can't go out."

"Danny, have you ever before known your dad to check on *Evie* without you and your brothers?"

"Why sure. The *Evie* is how we make our money." Danny relaxed.

"You have testified that lobster fishermen use an ice pick as a tool to mend traps. Have you ever, in your time fishing with your dad lost or misplaced the tool onboard?"

"When we're working on shore during off-season they don't go missing much. But when we are out at sea and the swell is shaking us we lose 'em. But they're cheap, four, five bucks. Dad replaces them when we're ashore."

"So you weren't surprised that you couldn't find the ice pick onboard when the investigator asked? Even now in season?"

"Hell no. Didn't think twice about it."

"No more questions." Alan had not moved from his seat.

The next witness was sworn in. Jimmy Moore looked terrified. Erin was aware that his witness feared Leland Boutilier. Jimmy was a credible witness. He was sober on the night of the murder and as a local fellow, he knew the players involved.

"Mr. Moore, may I call you Jimmy?"

"That's okay by me."

"Jimmy, you help out the people of this community by giving them a ride home if they can't drive safely themselves. Is that correct?"

"That's right. Sooner see them home safe than hurting anyone else or themselves."

"Are Leland Boutilier and his sons frequent users of your service?"

"Yes. Leland and I go way back. Known him since we were kids. He calls me all the time since he had trouble a few years back. He makes sure he and the boys get home safe."

"Would you say you and he are friends?"

"We don't hang out with the same crowd. I quit drinking years ago after my wife died in a car accident when I was driving."

"I'm sorry for your loss."

"I paid for it. Still do every night I crawl into bed alone."

"Jimmy, you came to pick up Leland and his sons on the night of March 16th this year. Please tell the court what occurred after you parked outside Pat Murphy's that night."

"Like I told the detective, I had to drive around the Bay from Black Point so I was a bit late, like it was about ten-thirty. Leland jumped in the front seat of my bus and the boys got in the back. Beth came out and yelled that she needed help. I went in. Leland came too, even though I told him not to. Beth was over by the guy at the bar and she was pretty upset. Leland went to go over to the bar but Beth scared us off when she screamed not to touch anything. She told me to call the cops."

"Please describe the man at the bar."

"I couldn't see his face but he had dirty white hair and a gray beard, I could see that much. He had his head on the bar. He wasn't moving none. I couldn't figure out why Beth was so crazy until I looked down on the floor. There was a pool of dark stuff. Usually when a guy like that has pissed himself the place smells like it. Then I got it. That was his blood on the floor."

"You say you have known Leland for many years. Did you also know his family?"

"Yes. I remember when he and Susie got married. Then they had Brandy. I was still drinking then. Trent, Leon's brother was in my class at school. Susie and Leon were older than us."

"Yet you didn't recognize Leon as the man dead at the bar on March 16th?"

"I didn't. Hadn't seen him since before he went to Dorchester for rapin' Brandy. Last time I saw him was when I bought some blow from him in Halifax twenty some odd years ago. Brandy was singing that night. I remember that. You say that was him that was murdered but I remember him as dark haired and a snappy dresser. He used to party hard."

"On the drive to West Dover the night of March 16th can you tell the court what you heard of the conversation in your vehicle?"

"Like I told that detective fella, the boys were liquored up. Leland was mouthing off as usual. Danny was full too. They were laughing about some guy they knew at the docks earlier. The roads were bad so I didn't pay their drunk talk much never mind."

"Jimmy, are you afraid of Leland Boutilier?"

"Oh Yeah. I told the detective that too. Leland's nasty when he gets loaded. Even sober I don't trust him. No secret; everyone knows that."

"Thank you Jimmy." Erin took his seat.

Alan Jones rose.

"Mr. Moore, after your wife died did you ask Leland Boutilier for a job on his boat?"

"Yes I did."

"Did he hire you?"

"No."

"Did you attend Mr. and Mrs. Boutilier's wedding?"

"No. I wasn't invited."

"Really? Mr. Moore were you in love with Susie Mason?"

"That was a long time ago. I was a kid with a crush. What's that got to do with anything now?"

"Mr. Moore, did you show up uninvited at her wedding reception?"

"I was drunk that night."

"Yes or no?"

"Yes."

"Did you spend the night in jail for attacking Leland Boutilier that night?"

"Yes. But like I said, that was a long time ago. That prick got her pregnant and her old man made her marry him. He never deserved her."

"No more questions." Alan sat.

Jimmy left the stand and looked longingly at Susie seated behind Leland. She met his eyes with a look of compassionate.

"We'll take a brief recess and reconvene in one hour. The jury is excused until then." Justice Weldon announced.

*   *   *

In the hall outside the courtroom Beth whispered in Eli's ear, "Holy shit!"

"Let's take a walk. You hungry?" Eli took Beth's arm and headed out the glass doors onto the concrete mezzanine. Ali and Amanda followed.

"No, I'm not hungry but I could use a coffee. *Perks* is close. Girls, are you coming?" Beth was flushed.

"We'll take a walk on the boardwalk instead. See who we can freak out." Amanda answered. "Come on Ali. It'll be fun."

Amanda was none the worse for having served her time. In fact, she accomplished another goal. She was served with a subpoena to appear at this trial as a witness while in jail. She was delighted. Her plan was coming together.

Eli was amazed. "They seem to have bonded."

"I still think Amanda is pretty superficial with all of us. I doubt that she would be here at all except that she is on the witness list. She'll never miss an opportunity to be a prima donna." Beth sipped her coffee. "So is a trial always like this?"

"No. This is going more quickly than most."

"I had no idea. Jones tries to discredit Mr McIsaac's witnesses and I assume the reverse will be true. Eli, I don't know if I can hold it together when that lawyer goes at me about my past. I will have to say that I did recognize that animal and so misled your early questioning."

"Beth you can only tell the truth. Just keep your answers short. You heard how both Danny and Jimmy didn't do that."

"I'm scared Eli. If Leland did this as you think he did, what if something I say makes the jury think I committed murder?"

"That won't happen. You didn't murder anyone. Relax." But Eli was not relaxed. He saw where Jones was going. Usually the crime investigators were called first. Eli was trying to understand Erin McIsaac's approach to this case.

The couple sat in silence with their own thoughts as they watched the ferry cross Halifax Harbour.

*   *   *

Jenna Renoldz was sworn in the Crown's next witness.

"Mrs. Reynoldz do you describe yourself as very observant person with a keen memory?"

"Yes."

"You and your husband, Adam were present in Pat Murphy's Pub on the evening Leon Mason was murdered. Is that correct?"

"Yes."

"What time did you arrive there?"

"Twenty minutes past eight."

"What did you observe?"

"As we entered a man at the bar said to the barmaid that he was buying a round for the house. The crowd that had been clustered there dispersed to tables. A large screen television on the back wall was tuned to the Weather Channel. The volume was too loud for my liking. I estimate that in the vicinity of thirty people, mostly men were in the establishment."

"So as the crowd thinned out did you see who was sitting at the bar?"

"An elderly, unkempt chap took the stool at the end by the wall; Amanda my husband's cousin took the seat beside him chatting the old fellow up; the man who bought the round was next and Adam pulled out the last stool for me."

"How long did you stay at Pat Murphy's that evening?"

"An hour and a bit. We left at nine-thirty. I was not very comfortable there."

"During that time what, if any observations did you make about the elderly man seated at the end of the bar?"

"He was in a quiet conversation with Amanda. I couldn't hear what was being said. He appeared to be getting very drunk. He raised his voice and the fellow sitting next to me told him to keep it down. Amanda left soon after."

"Did you happen to notice who took over Amanda's seat?"

"Yes. The man on trial, Leland Boutilier took the seat."

"Thank you Mrs. Reynoldz."

Alan Jones spoke, "I have no questions, at this time."

Jenna left the stand.

"The Crown calls Elizabeth Johnston."

"Ms Johnston, do you have any objection to me addressing you as Beth?"

"None whatsoever."

"For the record, you own and operate Pat Murphy's Pub in Indian Harbour. Is that correct?"

"I do."

"And you were working at your establishment on the evening of March 16 this year?"

"I was."

"What time do you announce 'last call' indicating that the pub is closing shortly?"

"At ten." Beth was doing her upmost to give short answers.

"And you did so on the night Leon Mason was murdered?"

"I did."

"There was quite a bad storm that night. Did you have many orders for 'last call'?"

"No."

"Please be more specific Beth."

"I had only one order. But other customers were at the bar impatient to settle up their bills."

"And who placed the last order?"

"Leland came to the bar for a jug, as he usually does at last call."

"Leland Boutilier?"

"Yes."

"Do you recall who else was at the bar at the time?"

"Like I said other customers and the man sitting at the end stool."

"And do you recall the condition man who we know was Leon, the victim?"

"He appeared to have fallen asleep."

"And Mr. Boutilier stood next to him?"

"He did."

"When Leland Boutilier left that night, did he make any comment to you?"

"Yes. He said, 'Messy guy you got left there! Let me know if you need help.'"

"What did you interpret that to mean?"

"That the fellow had passed out and urinated. Leland was offering to help me get the man on his feet to leave."

"Did you take his offer?"

"No."

"Why was that?"

"I can usually get that type of drunk going by myself."

"Any other reason?"

"I didn't want any trouble."

"Meaning what?"

"Leland and his sons have caused, well, I've seen them be a little heavy handed when they're drinking too much."

"Beth, a previous witness testified that you did ask for help. Why did you change your mind?"

"When I couldn't rouse the guy as I usually can, I went outside to get Jimmy. I thought that if he and I could bring the man around I could pour some coffee into him and have Jimmy take him to wherever he was staying."

"But that did not happen. Why was that?"

"When I came back inside and went around the bar, I realized the puddle on the floor wasn't urine. I saw that he was dead. I got Jimmy to call the police."

"Thank you Ms Johnston."

Alan Jones slowly approached the witness stand. Beth was more anxious than she thought she would be.

"When questioned by the RCMP detectives on the night of the murder did you lie in any of your answers?"

"Yes."

"Please elaborate."

"I said I did not know the victim."

"So you did know Leon Mason?"

"I encountered him once before, many years ago. So I did not strictly speaking, 'know' him. I only recognized his face at the end of the night."

"What were the circumstances under which, as you describe, 'encountered' him?"

"In April of 1986 he raped me."

"Was he charged with that crime?"

"No."

"Today we have heard testimony that Leon Mason was alive at nine-thirty. You have stated 'under oath' that at last call Leon Mason 'appeared to have fallen asleep' and that he refused help 'to get him on his feet'."

"Your Worship, does my colleague intend to ask a question?" Erin asked.

"Pick up the pace Mr. Jones. Ask your question or move on." Judge Weldon looked over his glasses at Defense Counsel.

Beth spoke, "I did not testify that the man refused help."

Alan Jones ignored her comment, Erin did not object. Surprised by a missed opportunity to make a point Alan continued his cross-examination. "Ms Johnston, how long were you alone with the man who you claim raped you?"

"I'm sorry. I don't understand the question." Beth was beginning to show her anxiety.

"Let me rephrase then. On March 16th, after the bar emptied, how long were you alone with the man at the bar whom you recognized as the man who supposedly raped you?"

Beth was fighting back the tears. She did not rise to the debate being offered. Jones' next questions would be worse. When she sent Jimmy away that night to take Leland and the boys home she knew she was making a mistake.

"When I went out to ask for Jimmy for help, I had not yet realized . . ."

"Please answer my question Ms Johnston."

"Maybe five minutes. But as I tried to say . . ."

"And as I understand, after closing there is a certain amount of cleaning up to be done. Is that correct?" Alan Jones wore no expression on his face.

"Yes but . . ."

"Do you wear gloves when you do that cleanup?"

"Yes."

"And did you convince Jimmy Moore to take the Boutiliers home leaving you alone to wait for the RCMP?"

"Yes." Beth felt her courage and stamina draining away.

"So again, how long were you alone with the man who supposedly raped you, who was known to be alive less than an hour before, who only you had decided was not sleeping but was," he paused, "dead."

Defeated and empty Beth whispered, "Fifteen minutes."

Erin McIsaac jumped to his feet. "Objection. Mr Jones is badgering this witness!"

"Question asked and answered but I agree Mr McIsaac. Be very careful Mr Jones." Judge Weldon warned.

"I understand. And I have only one more question". Annoyed that his momentum was interrupted, Alan lowered his voice. He did not change the smug look on his face when he spoke. "Do you take medication for anxiety; in fact the same medication found in the victim's blood?"

"Yes." Beth broke.

Through her sobs, the pain from years of fear and hatred released. At last.

"That is all I have for this witness at this time." Back in his seat Alan quickly glanced toward the jury and was shocked. The Foreman's eyes were full of disgust and fixed on him.

"Court is adjourned. The jury will be sequestered." The judge announced. "We will reconvene at nine tomorrow morning."

* * *

"That was brutal." Ali said to Amanda as she drove out of the parking lot. "Should we go back to Beth's place?"

"No, I say we head to Pat Murphy's." Amanda answered. "I need a drink." She was thinking about her own testimony. She understood the defense lawyer's tactics. She planned to use the witness box as a stage. The press would love her.

"I had no idea Beth used pills for anxiety. Maybe it's genetic. I use them too. I think I'm dying when I get a panic attack. What about you? You've spent enough time with shrinks." Ali was thinking out loud.

"Yeah, whatever. I don't want to talk. Just drive Ali."

* * *

The foreman of the jury, Jake Bolden, sat on his bed with his head in his hands. He decided not to join the others for dinner, preferring to call on 'room service'. He was appalled by the cross examination and the obnoxious attitude of the defense lawyer. His emotional reaction stirred memories of another court case more than fifty years before. He watched his father be humiliated, his integrity attacked and his vibrant spirit broken. The trial became a mockery of the judicial system in which his father passionately believed. Walter Bolden was found not guilty of fraud but his law practice and reputation were destroyed.

Jake was apprehensive a month ago when he received the notice to appear for jury duty. He expected not to be chosen as a juror. Jake lived a comfortable life in the south end of Halifax, enjoyed a successful career and looked forward to a pleasant retirement. He did not consider himself to be a 'peer' of the accused. Now having been elected as Foreman, the experience was becoming a nightmare.

*   *   *

"Jenna, you were so good today. I was really proud of how you handled the questions." Adam made the effort to engage his wife in dinner conversation.

"Adam don't you dare patronize me. Did you hear that awful Jones fellow say *'I have no questions, at this time'*? That means I may have to testify again. I am so embarrassed by all of this. My parents don't know what to say to their friends. God knows the press coverage. The press could ruin my business. " Jenna was not in the mood to talk. "This is all your fault for lying to me."

*   *   *

Leland's demeanor did not impress the guards as they secured him in his cell.

But his cellmate was comfortable enough to ask, "How'd it go today?"

"My lawyer kicked butt man! Didn't think he had the parts when I first met him but he did today. I'm gettin' off. Mark my words, my friend. That bitch Beth Johnston did the deed. I'll be a free man soon enough! Mark my words."

*   *   *

The following morning shone bright with the colourful autumn light falling over St Margaret's Bay. To avoid the morning traffic Eli and Beth started out early on their way to Halifax.

"You don't have to go today Beth. I could take you home, there's time."

"I'm going Eli. I had a good sleep, thanks to you. My worst fear about being a witness is passed. No one arrested me. And I need to be there. You will likely testify. I see your own anxiety and that's because of me. We talked about that."

"You know Jaime, or Bruce, whatever his name is may be called today. Can you cope with seeing him and listening to what he might say especially after what Jones put you through yesterday?"

"Yes. And if Amanda is called I can hear her version too. I had a weak moment yesterday. Okay. I'm over it. Besides, I can't wait to hear Leland answer Erin's cross if we get that far today."

*   *   *

The trial resumed precisely on time. The lead coroner, Dr Evelyn Donaldson was on the witness stand for the Crown.

"Dr Donaldson, in you investigation of this case were you able to determine the time of victim's time of death?"

"The coroner who assessed the victim on site determined that death occurred within the hour previous to his arrival which was at ten forty-five pm on March 16, 2011."

"At autopsy were you able to determine the cause of death?"

"I was. Death resulted as a single stab wound to the left side of the chest. I removed an ice pick from the site. The wound resulted in a pneumothorax, in other words, a collapsed lung. Such an event causes compromise to the heart. In this case toxicology also demonstrated the presence of potentially cardio toxic and respiratory depressant chemicals which weakened his body's defenses."

"Thank you Dr Donaldson."

Alan Jones shook his head as he stood. "I don't know about the members of the jury but I had difficulty understanding what you have told us Dr. Donaldson. Help me here. I understand, from what you've testified that Leon Mason died between nine and ten forty-five and that the ice pick you removed from his chest, when he was stabbed with it, was the beginning of the end for Leon Mason's life. Do I understand correctly?"

"Essentially, yes."

"Would having an ice pick thrust into a person's chest cause pain; cause a person to cry out?"

"Usually, yes. In this case, not necessarily."

"I'm confused again Dr Donaldson. Please help me, and the jury to understand."

"First of all, the man had been drinking alcohol. The level in his blood was twice the level to legally drive. His blood also showed significant amounts of cannabis, cocaine as well as benzodiazepines, in particular Ativan. The combination would dull any pain."

"Thank you. That helps my understanding of his condition as the circumstances under which he died." Alan Jones wrung his hands as he walked up and down before the jury. He turned and stared at the witness. "I get all that. I understand the why and when of the time of death. What I still don't understand is, how long does it take someone to die after being stabbed? Can you help us with that?"

Dr Donaldson looked down at her hands folded tightly on her knees. "That depends on a number of factors."

"That's not particularly helpful Dr Donaldson. Then let me ask you this. How much effort would you say it takes to push an ice pick into a comatose man slumped over a bar?"

"That depends on the strength of the person who has the intent to kill the man."

Alan Jones decided not to push further with his questions. He was satisfied and threw up his hands theatrically. "No more questions."

Erin called Brandy Boutilier as his next witness. Alan Jones was expecting the Crown to call Detective Connors followed by Bruce Matthews and complete their witness roster with Brandy.

"Ms Boutilier on the night your uncle, Leon Boutilier raped you was he carrying a weapon?"

"Yes. He had an ice pick in his hand."

"Something like this?" Erin picked up the murder weapon and held up the bag for the jury to see clearly.

"Yes."

"On the day Leon Mason was sentenced do you recall your father's final words to him?"

"Yes, he said he would kill Leon when he got out of prison."

"No more questions. Thank you Ms Boutilier. Your witness."

Alan Jones declined to cross-examine. Instead he requested a brief recess.

* * *

Nothing about Brandy's testimony was unexpected. Knowing she was the Crown's key witness Alan had planned a rhythm to his cross-examinations. Not having the opportunity to fully expose Connors' relationship with Beth Johnston robbed him of the chance to challenge the validity of the entire investigation. His strategy was damaged. He was aware of the impact Brandy's testimony had on the jury. Alan thought carefully. He would push Bruce Matthews harder than initially intended.

* * *

Bruce Matthews took the witness stand.

Erin began, "Mr. Matthews, were you present at Pat Murphy's Pub on the evening Leon Mason was murdered?"

"I was, yes."

"Previous testimony given to the Court places you seated at the bar beside Leland Boutilier at nine-thirty. Is that correct?"

"Yes."

"Was there a conversation going on between Leland and the man seated next to him, Leon Mason?"

"Yes. But I couldn't hear what was said. Leland ordered beer and when Beth was pouring Leland gave the man a shove. He laughed, spilled a bit of his beer and staggered back to his table."

"What, if anything did you observe about Leon's condition after the incident?"

"That's difficult to answer. A couple of men moved in so my view of Leon was obscured. All I can say is when I left he had his head down on the bar."

"What time did you leave Pat Murphy's?"

"Well, before last call, so about ten to ten."

"Thank you. Your witness Mr. Jones."

"Mr. Matthews, I notice you speak of those involved in this trial in a very familiar manner, as if you were referring to family. Please comment."

"Several of them are. Leland Boutilier is my uncle, as was Leon Mason. I legally changed my name when I moved to British Columbia twenty-five years ago. That may be confusing to you."

"I'm sure that helps the jury to understand your familiarity. I understand that you returned to Nova Scotia in March to settle your mother's estate. Is that correct?"

"Yes."

"You now own the family home on Mackerel Point Road, yet you chose to stay at the Harbour Inn. Why is that Mr. Matthews?"

"Objection—relevance." Erin spoke.

"I'll allow the question." Judge Weldon gave the defense the latitude to proceed. "Please answer Mr. Matthews."

"Comfort reasons only. The house was cold."

"Really. Past memories played no part? Never mind. Tell us then how you came to be at Pat Murphy's Pub that night."

"I wanted to see Beth Johnston."

"I see. You and she were romantically involved as teens. Is that true?"

"Yes. But we hadn't spoken for many years. She didn't recognize me this March. I've gotten older and she was preoccupied. My uncles didn't know me either. But I didn't expect them to."

"Help me understand. You were seated at the bar beside your uncle, Leland Boutilier who was seated beside your other uncle, Leon Mason and in front of your old girlfriend Beth Johnston. Yet you did not tell any of these people who you were?"

"I didn't care about Leland. I never liked the man. I cared less about Leon. I was focused on Beth. I kept hoping she would realize it was me."

"Thank you. Interesting." Alan needed to cautiously choose his words. "Now, not only had your appearance changed but your Uncle Leon, as you knew him, was different. Yet you did recognize him. When and under what circumstances did you last see him?"

"I remember the day clearly Mr. Jones. In fact, every morning since I wake with the memory before me." Jaime's voice was strong. "On the afternoon of Sunday, April 27th, 1986 I saw Leon Mason raping Beth Johnston."

Every member of the jury gasped. Alan Jones could not have been more pleased. He was convinced now that he would be able to provide the jury with grounds for 'reasonable doubt'. His hunch was correct. One more question he hoped would seal the verdict.

"That must have been shocking for you. Do you need to take a moment?"

"No. I'm good. Carry on." Bruce's eyes locked with Beth's. "I want this over."

"Was your uncle using a weapon to restrain her?"

"It was my ice pick."

"As a mechanic, is that a tool you continue to use?"

"Yes."

"Mr. Matthews, did you want Leon Mason dead?"

"I've been waiting for someone to ask me that question." Bruce sat forward. "More than anything I wanted him to die. He ruined my life and those of the people I loved. I backed down from my responsibility in the past. I paid dearly for that. On March 16th the opportunity to have him pay with his life was there in front of me. That night I made sure he could never hurt anyone again. I was proud to drive that ice pick into his chest. Unfortunately he was already unconscious and not able to experience the terror of dying."

EPILOGUE

Beth Johnston

Not merely satisfied, Beth now thoroughly enjoys her life. Having the opportunity to know her family delights Beth more than she ever could have imagined.

Pat Murphy's Pub continues as the hub of Indian Harbour. Business thrives throughout all seasons.

Eli is her lover and best friend.

Her nightmare disappeared.

Eli Connors

Detective Connors considers himself very fortunate. The department reprimanded him for his inappropriate liaison with Beth Johnston during the murder investigation of Leon Mason. The matter ended there.

Eli plans to propose marriage during the couple's vacation.

Bruce Matthews

On September 21, 2011 Bruce Matthews immediately was taken into custody after confessing to the murder of Leon Mason. At arraignment he entered a plea of 'Guilty'. Before sentencing he made the following allocution:

"I killed Leon Mason and have no regret for doing so. My only regret is betraying and abandoning the love of my life twenty-five years ago."

He was sentenced to life imprisonment.

Elizabeth Johnston was not in the courtroom.

Adam Reynoldz

Jenna had Adam served with divorce papers shortly after the trial.

Adam's land development project is beginning construction. Sylvie lives happily with her father on the Aspotogan Peninsula. She sees her mother occasionally.

Adam and Sylvie visit Auntie Beth every Wednesday night for supper.

Leland Boutilier

With his sons Danny, Scott and Paul, the captain and crew of *Evie* continue to be the last to leave Pat Murphy's Pub after last call. Jimmy Moore drives them home.

They all still debate the night of March 16th, 2011.

Alison McLaughlin

Now based in Nova Scotia, Ali continues her career in Photojournalism. When home in Indian Harbour, she keeps company with Erin McIsaac.

Her nightmare continues. She intends to find her sister.

Amanda Stewart

Amanda left the Halifax courtroom on September 21, 2011 as Bruce Matthews confessed to the murder of Leon Mason. She walked to the rental car parked on Hollis Street and left the city. A twelve-hour drive to the private clinic in Quebec gave Amanda plenty of time to think, and to plan. She recognized the mistake she made by not including Bruce Matthews in the family reunion on March 16. She vowed not to make such an omission in the future.

Six months later, Amanda Stewart, now Alexandra Sullivan boarded a small aircraft. Fear of flying was the last remnant of her former self. Relaxing as the pills took effect, she settled into the seat beside a handsome middle-aged gentleman concentrating on the *Globe and Mail.* He did not recognize her.

For the last time Amanda opened her journal. On the final page she wrote:

March 2012

Last year I carefully planned the murder of Leon Mason. I knew he wouldn't resist my invitation. For

our family reunion I orchestrated the appearance of four
potential murderers; Beth, Adam, Alison and of course, me.
On March 16, 2011 I laced Leon's beer with enough benzos
to kill him. Bruce Matthews stole the glory by driving, of
all things, an ice pick into the bastard's chest and then
confessing to the crime. I was disappointed not to have my
chance to testify; my performance was to be a real thriller.
    Regardless, I am finished with that family.
    "Good-bye Amanda Stewart".

She closed the book. Shoving her past three years deep between the magazines in the seat pocket ahead, she beckoned a passing flight attendant.

"Scotch and water. Single malt if you have it." Alexandra knew she and the man seated beside her had more in common than drink preference.

Several hours later as the landing gear touched down, Alexandra smiled at Michael. "I am so pleased we met. The island is tiny. Perhaps our paths will cross again."